Old Bethlehem Christmas Mysteries

Book One

The Mystery Woman at Church and Main

Book Two

Who Stole the Wise Men?

Charlene Donchez Mowers

Carol A. Reifinger

Old Bethlehem Christmas Mysteries is a work of fiction.
The places are real, but their descriptions are not exact.

ISBN - 978-0-692-52933-1

Photos by Linda L. Wickmann
Graphic Design by Sandy Yoder

Printed in Bethlehem, Pennsylvania
November 2015
Christmas City Printing

TABLE OF CONTENTS

Acknowledgements v

Christmas in Bethlehem – A Picture Postcard vii

Book One   *The Mystery Woman at Church and Main*

    Chapter One - A Slippery Slope 1

    Chapter Two - Managing the Media 5

    Chapter Three - The Carriage Trade 9

    Chapter Four - Visit From a Wise Man 11

    Chapter Five - Spirits of Christmas Past 15

    Chapter Six - Bethlehem Histories 19

    Chapter Seven - 'Tis the Season .21

    Chapter Eight - Mind the Carriage, Sir! 25

    Chapter Nine - Dinner at the Shelter 27

    Chapter Ten - Clues at the Burnside Plantation 31

    Chapter Eleven - Treasure in the Walls 35

    Chapter Twelve - Just Another Evening in Bethlehem 39

    Chapter Thirteen - Still a Mystery 45

    Chapter Fourteen - A Christmas Open House 47

    Epilogue 51

Book Two   *Who Stole the Wise Men?*

    Chapter One - The Phone Call 55

    Chapter Two - A Package Arrives 57

    Chapter Three - Prepping for the Christmas Season 59

    Chapter Four - Thanksgiving, Already? 63

    Chapter Five - Back in Town 65

    Chapter Six - A Putz Watcher 69

    Chapter Seven - The Bus Ride 71

    Chapter Eight - Tickets are Needed 73

Chapter Nine - The Advent Lovefeast 75

Chapter Ten - The Buses Arrive 77

Chapter Eleven - A Tall Tale 83

Chapter Twelve - Missing Pieces 85

Chapter Thirteen - A Young Thief Confesses 87

Chapter Fourteen - Some Research to Do 89

Chapter Fifteen - Pieces of Silver 91

Chapter Sixteen - The Christmas Pageant 93

Chapter Seventeen - A New Day .97

Chapter Eighteen - The Police Report 99

Chapter Nineteen - A Very Merry Christmas 101

A Glossary of Moravian Terms 103

Appendices
Historic Bethlehem Museum & Sites 105

Historic Moravian Bethlehem .107

Central Moravian Church 109

Moravian Denomination 110

The Old Moravian Chapel 111

The Moravian Archives 112

Bethlehem Area Moravians, Inc. 113

For Further Reading 114

About the Authors 116

Map of Downtown Bethlehem 118

Aｆter our first book, *The Body in the Vat: Tales from the Tannery*, published in the Christmas season of 2014, a number of readers encouraged us to keep writing. Immersed as we were at the time in everything Christmas, we decided to write about the intriguing mysteries of Christmas in Bethlehem.

Once again, we need to acknowledge the wonderful institutions and people with whom we have worked over the many years of our professional lives. The top notch Board members of Historic Bethlehem Museums & Sites who lead the organization continue to inspire us with their love of Bethlehem and their dedication to preserving its history. The pastors and Joint Board of Central Moravian Church work faithfully and well to carry out the mission of the Church within the community and in the world. We are grateful for the support of both organizations and dedicate this book to them.

Christmas in Bethlehem – A Picture Postcard

JUST as the orange sun begins to set and bare-branched trees reach out like black paper cut-outs against the sky, lighted candles begin to glow warmly in the windows of every building in the old Moravian district, as well as in the homes of many of the residents of the city of Bethlehem, Pennsylvania. Twenty-six pointed Moravian stars shine in doorways, each with a soft, steady light cutting through the darkness to illumine the way for the coming of the Christ Child.

The majestic sounds of choir and organ pour from Central Moravian Church on these evenings, as rehearsals and concerts, vespers and Advent services fill the large sanctuary many times over during the season.

Gathered under street lights, visitors huddling against the cold listen intently to costumed tour guides dressed in simple colonial garb. The story of the city's founding on Christmas Eve in 1741 charms and captivates seekers of the true Christmas spirit.

Away from the bustling crowds on Main Street, just a block away at the Christian Education Building, volunteers welcome visitors who come to see the Central Moravian Church Christmas Putz. "Each year," the greeters recount, "members of our Church travel to the Poconos, where they gather fresh moss. They bring it back and place the moss on a raised wooden platform and then carefully arrange the Nativity figures on top of it." The Putz curtain opens and once again, each year, the story of the birth of Jesus is told with recorded narration, music and antique figures nestled in the moss. Just steps away, the Single Sisters' House on Church Street is home to several smaller, lovingly arranged putzes, one in each of the rooms formerly inhabited by single women throughout the years.

Beautiful, quiet, lovely traditions wrap the city in a humble embrace, and time seems to stop for a moment or two. Bethlehem becomes a gentle, old-fashioned picture postcard.

Soft and sentimental brushstrokes blend together to depict a peaceful town that cherishes its noble history. But be assured, dear reader, that beneath the quaint vignettes, dark mysteries spread across the canvas...

Old Bethlehem Christmas Mysteries

Book One

The Mystery Woman at Church and Main

CHAPTER ONE

Docent - A tour guide; a woman or man who interprets history for visitors.

"A Slippery Slope"

ON a sunny afternoon in early December, the corner of Main and Church Streets in Bethlehem resembled a German outdoor market, with crowds pushing toward the row of wooden booths filled with candles and soaps, woolen shawls and sparkling crystal ornaments. Mitzi and Adele made their way past the line of people waiting for horse and carriage rides and stood for a moment near the booth selling fragrant soaps. The women were tempted to stop and browse for a bit, but they knew that the afternoon was scheduled down to the last minute. They had just finished a book signing at the Book Shop and were headed up the hill to Central Church's Christian Education Building. The CE Building was the home for the community's Christmas Putz, a Nativity display that the congregation assembled lovingly every year. The building was also home to the Star & Candle Shoppe, a gift shop that Adele had started several years ago.

Before they could round the corner to the steps leading to the Church Green, an exasperated looking woman nearby called out to a friend, "What is a "Putz" anyway?" Her friend, catching the hand of the small child by her side laughed and replied, "I don't know *what* it is, but I know *where* it is. It's in the CE Building, just up this hill!"

Without saying a word, Adele and Mitzi both smiled and made the quick decision not to get involved in the conversation they overheard this time, figuring that once the women got to the building, they would find out what a Putz was and would get to experience it firsthand.

Mitzi, as President of the Bethlehem Historical Society and Adele, as Pastor of Central Moravian Church, each answered a myriad of questions during the Advent and Christmas seasons. They retold the story of the founding of Bethlehem; they described the purpose of the large stone

1

buildings that lined Church Street; they even made suggestions for lunch or dinner at nearby restaurants. Each felt that hospitality was part of what the Christmas City was all about.

Invariably though, some misinformation was bound to get out. Strange things like, "There are no more living Moravians," or, "The Moravian Sisters were nuns who lived in a convent."

Mitzi was especially concerned about the accuracy of what her guides, or docents, shared with the public. The docents all had training and were conscientious about following through on the more difficult questions that tourists asked. But from time to time, some very unusual, whisper-down-the-alley tidbits started circulating. So whenever she could, Mitzi met with the docents to reinforce with them the true story of the early Moravians.

"That's an intense group over there," Adele said as they finally reached the top of the steps to Heckewelder Place. She motioned to a small circle of people gathered around a docent in colonial dress who was pointing quite animatedly to the Church belfry. "They're really listening to your docent."

"I'm not sure who that docent is," said Mitzi, squinting at the group on the far corner of the Green. "She could be one of the new people that we hired this fall. If we had more time I would go over and say "hi." "

"But we don't really have time today," Adele chimed in quickly, steering her toward the CE Building. "Our husbands are waiting, and probably not too patiently at this point."

Adele's husband, Zeke, was coming into town to join her and Mitzi and Vaughn for dinner. They were to meet in the Star and Candle Shoppe parking lot.

"I hope that we can..." began Mitzi, stopping abruptly in her tracks. "What's going on at the Nain House? Do you see a police cruiser?" She quickly climbed the small set of steps leading to the second level of the Church Green, straining to see what was happening up on Heckewelder Place, the narrow street leading into Church Street.

"Looks like police *and* fire trucks," observed Adele, following Mitzi.

"I'm going over to see what the problem is. Go on ahead and I'll catch up when I can." She turned and went directly to the Nain House, a small cottage that the Historical Society had moved to this location. It once housed native Americans and was one of the few structures remaining from their early community. The restoration had just been completed and Mitzi hoped that the flurry of excitement today was just another false alarm related to the still to be resolved construction glitches.

"I'll meet you in a few minutes," Adele said. "Call my cell if you get held up."

Mitzi was already striding across the Green that was still covered with a light coating of snow and ice from last week's storm. Adele shook her head and wondered where Mitzi got the energy to be so involved in every property that the Society oversaw, 20 buildings and sites altogether. There were continual challenges in caring for old historic properties, as Adele knew well herself, having worked for so long with the governing Boards of Central Moravian Church to care for the buildings on its campus. The headaches went with the territory. But not for a minute would she or Mitzi think of giving up on the wonderful old treasures they helped to protect.

As Adele opened the door to the CE Building, two Candle Shoppe volunteers were standing by ready to pounce. "We're glad to see you," said the woman closest to the door. "We have a situation that you need to hear about." So for the next twenty minutes or so, Adele dealt with an older member of the congregation who insisted that she had left her purchases with the cashier at the Shoppe and now they were gone. Finally, Adele said quietly to the cashier, "Just go head and replace the purchases. If we happen to find the ones that she said that we lost, we'll just put them back on the tables." Sometimes the pastoral thing to do was the best, she thought. And it certainly went along with "The customer is always right" motto.

As she was dealing with the disgruntled shopper, Adele could see out of the corner of her eye that Zeke and Vaughn had already arrived and were circling, waiting to meet her and Mitzi to go to dinner. They were either being very patient or didn't want to get involved with the shopper fracas.

"Hi there, you two. I'll bet you thought we'd never show up for dinner," Adele teased. "We just have to wait for Mitzi to get back from the Nain House. There was some kind of emergency over there."

"We saw the ambulance, " said Vaughn, "and figured that something had happened."

"Ambulance? The police were there, and a fire truck, but not an ambulance..." Just as Adele walked over to peer out the window toward the Green, her cell phone rang. It was Mitzi.

Before her friend could speak, Adele said excitedly, "Hey Mitzi, the guys said that they saw an ambulance on Heckewelder. Is anyone hurt?"

"Yes ... me!" exclaimed Mitzi, clearly shaken. "I just finished talking with the police about the false alarm and left to come up to the CE building to meet you when I fell on a patch of ice. It was a good thing that the docent we saw earlier was coming down the walk next to the Church and saw me, or I'd still be lying there behind a tree. She called the ambulance. She was wearing her cape with the hood up, so I couldn't really see her face."

"Are you alright?"

"Apparently I sprained my ankle pretty badly, but otherwise I'm okay. The paramedics are just finishing with me now, but I need some help to walk. Is Vaughn there? Could you send him down to Heckewelder to pick me up?"

"We're on our way, kid. Stay put!"

Within minutes, they all arrived on Heckewelder and Mitzi was safely transferred from the ambulance to Vaughn's car, and they were on their way home.

Adele took a deep breath and turned to Zeke. "That's enough excitement for one day."

"Does this mean that we're not going to dinner?" asked Zeke, grimacing.

"It means that you're grilling tonight on the patio," said Adele, getting into the car. "Sounds good to me, " said Zeke, "Never too cold to grill."

CHAPTER TWO

Managing the Media

HER ankle was a little uncomfortable for a day or two, but Mitzi decided to ignore it and have Vaughn drive her to the office. The Christmas season was no time for rest, even with an injury.

Her first order of business was to try to reach the young woman docent who helped her by calling the ambulance. But no one in the office seemed to know who she was when Mitzi described her.

"Let's take a look at the current roster of docents, " Mitzi said. "If she is new to us this season, we can at least get a name." Her assistant brought in a long list of docents for the season.

After looking over the list, Mitzi realized that although there may have been new people on the list, she could identify each person; either she knew them socially or they had volunteered in the past. It was a total mystery who the docent was. It was a shame that Mitzi couldn't thank the young woman personally.

Odd though, she thought. There were comments coming in to the office almost every day about this terrific docent who was so helpful and knowledgeable, and who went out of her way to make people feel welcome. Was she the same woman Mitzi encountered? Who was this person? And, how could I clone her, she thought with a smile. Here was a person who was a great ambassador for the city, and for the Historical Society, as well.

The knock on her office door startled her. Adele came in, gave Mitzi a quick hug and then dropped into the chair across from Mitzi's desk. She took off her knit hat, fluffed her brown hair and said, "Back already! Vaughn said you were in the office today. How's the ankle?"

"Not bad, really. There was just no way that I could stay at home. It's just too hectic around here."

"No point in arguing with you. You're as stubborn as I am. By the way, did you ever figure out who helped you the other day?"

"I'm working on it, but honestly Adele, I have no idea who the person was. None of my staff can guess either."

"At least this mystery person is not as sinister as our stalker Norman Sterner was." Sterner was the nefarious antiques collector and thief who had threatened them at gunpoint in the old Tannery last fall. They were relieved that he was apprehended and was now incarcerated.

"I don't even want to think about Sterner. This woman is more like some anonymous angel. Did I tell you that I've been getting reports about this docent who is just so incredibly good?"

"I've been hearing about her too. Some members of the congregation came to me to say that they were with friends from out of town and how much they enjoyed being with such a wonderful guide. We've got to figure out who she is!"

"I think we need to put that investigation on hold for now," Mitzi said. "You and I really need to talk about our interview with the TV network this Thursday."

"I've been pondering that," Adele sighed. "We know how it goes. We spend so much time with the camera crew and interviewer and then when all is said and done, we get less than a minute of air time. We've been around this block before."

"Yes, we have, but I think it's still worth the effort. The Tourism Office is really doing its best to get the city more exposure, and this interview is kind of a coup when you think about the possibility of getting our story on the evening news."

"Of course you're right, Mitzi. We've gotten such great feedback from the pieces that they've done in the past. I'm going to stay optimistic, I promise. So let's talk over what is going to happen. And first of all, what are you going to wear?"

"I thought about wearing colonial dress myself, but decided against it. We don't want to perpetuate the myth that Moravians are Amish.

I think I'll wear something warm, probably a sweater and wool skirt and that bright red scarf that Vaughn gave me, with my long charcoal coat. It is an outdoor interview, after all."

"Where will we be set up? I hope we can be in a spot that shows the Church Green and the Christmas booths, as well as the shops on Main Street."

"We can certainly suggest that. I just hope that the weather cooperates."

"I do too. Well, I've got to run. By coincidence, I have a meeting with the Church Communications Committee this afternoon. They'll be excited to hear more about our TV coverage. I'm sure that several committee people will just *happen* to be walking by when we go live."

Just then a staff person knocked on the door and the phone rang at the same time, so Adele smiled, waved goodbye and bundled up against the cold. "See you later," she mouthed to Mitzi.

CHAPTER THREE

The Carriage Trade

BY the time Adele walked up the long hill behind the Hotel from Mitzi's office, she was warm as toast. She crossed Main Street, eying the slow, plodding white horse-drawn carriage pulling up near the entrance to the Green. I've never actually been on a carriage ride around town, she thought. Maybe this year, if she could convince Zeke to go along.

She glanced at the two passengers getting ready to step down to the sidewalk from the carriage and was surprised to see Sally Marshall and her husband Chris. Sally, the *Reverend* Sally Marshall, was a new pastor on Adele's staff. The Church Boards had approved of the idea of calling Sally as a second full-time pastor, especially since their part-timer, a retired former pastor, the Rev. Dr. Baxter Hemphill, wanted to cut back his hours. Not that Baxter was slowing down. In fact, he was cutting back so he could focus on opening his ski shop on Broad Street.

Sally was a terrific addition to the staff: young, bright, energetic and eager to learn more about Bethlehem and to be a part of a team. Her husband, Chris, was a freelance graphic designer who had no problem finding clients in the Lehigh Valley.

"Doing the tourist thing?" teased Adele as she came around the carriage to greet Sally.

"Absolutely! What an interesting ride. I think Chris got some good ideas for sketches, too."

"Lots," Chris grinned. "Can I get you two pastors some hot chocolate? I'm headed into the Book Shop and deli."

"You and Sally go ahead," said Adele. "I'll take a rain check this time." It was too bad that she wasn't able to spend more time with Sally and introduce her to some people in the community, but Sally had just been installed at the Church, and at the beginning of a very busy season.

Adele made a mental note to set an appointment with Mitzi, so that they could introduce Sally to the work of the Historical Society. Mitzi met her briefly at Sally's reception, but they had little time together. Sally should also meet Beth Ettwein, and her fiancé Mark Sargent, two avid, young volunteers who helped Mitzi and Adele apprehend the dangerous stalker last fall.

Adele's walk down Heckewelder was brightened as the electric candles in each window of each building on campus were turned on. It was a lovely custom, more special because it was reserved for this one season. "Lighting the way for the baby Jesus," was how one of the children in Sunday School had described it.

As she approached the Church office, she saw a lone female figure in colonial garb, her dark cape and white haube clearly visible, walking quickly down Church Street toward the Single Brethren's House. Within seconds, she seemed to vanish. She's that mystery docent, thought Adele, frustrated that she didn't have time to run after her. The committee members were already at the door, waiting for Adele to unlock it for the meeting.

"On my way," she called to the committee, just as the belfry clock struck the hour.

CHAPTER FOUR

Visit from a Wise Man

THE afternoon sun filtered through the blinds behind her desk as Mitzi glanced at her watch. Her next appointment was with Fred Lang, a friend and long-time volunteer for the Society. Fred was always enthusiastic and just as willing to dig into old Bethlehem stories and do genealogical research as he was willing to scoop ice cream at the annual Blueberry Festival. Mitzi remembered well that it was Fred who helped to unravel the last mystery that she and Adele had tackled. His visit today was at Mitzi's request, because Fred was always a good resource and a sounding board for ideas.

There was a tap on the door and in came Fred, bearing a small bouquet of flowers. "Hope you're doing better, Boss," said Fred with a big smile."You know you should be at home, right?"

"I'm actually doing well, Fred. Thanks for coming in and thanks for the lovely flowers. I should get a sprained ankle more often!"

"Don't get used to the good treatment. I am really here to lobby for a little idea that I had for the television interview."

"Great! What did you have in mind?"

"You know how we usually bring just one costumed female docent to do this type of interview? I am proposing that we use a male docent this time, too, and let them both do the guided tour for the TV crew. And maybe do it from a slightly different perspective."

"Well, having a couple would be an interesting idea. But there is still the question of whether or not to have anyone at all dressed in colonial garb. On one hand, some of us talked about how important it is to help people understand that Bethlehem is not stuck in colonial days and that Moravians today are not like our plain dress Amish friends. But on the other hand, there are lots of ways to get that concept across. I think we should definitely have a colonial couple for the TV segment. But there is one condition."

"What's that?"

"You should be the male docent."

"Mitzi, you know I wasn't proposing that I do the interview..." demurred Fred, reddening and a little embarrassed by the thought.

"I understand, but you would be terrific. You know the history of Bethlehem as well as anyone and you've been a docent for us for years. Plus, you look good in a colonial hat."

"It always helps to flatter me. I think I might be able to do it justice, if you and I worked together on a script."

"That sounds great! Let's take a look at the schedule that the network sent us first, and try to decide how we want to plan the day. They'll have their own ideas, of course, but we need to be ready to make some suggestions. Adele is going to bring some ideas from the Church's Communication Committee, too." Wincing a bit as she stood up, Mitzi smoothed out the schedule sent to the Society by the network office. "Where do you think we should begin? Should we start at the Gemeinhaus or down on Main Street?"

"Well, I was thinking that when we tell the story of the founding of Bethlehem by Moravians in 1741, we might want to suggest that the cameras begin by filming a bit at the First House, over in the Rose Garden." Fred knew that the site of the real first house was now where the Hotel stood, but some footage of the rough replica in the Rose Garden would be good to include, if for no other reason than to show the small size of the log building that could have housed most of the people and livestock of the settlement at the time.

"Not that I think we should short-change the filming of the rest of the buildings in the historic district itself, but could we suggest that the crew do some shots of Burnside as well?" asked Fred.

Burnside was the farm to the northwest of the historic district that Moravian James Burnside built in 1747 on the banks of the Monocacy

Creek. The "plantation" as it was called, was beautifully decorated for Christmas and gave the appearance of a working farm.

"We can certainly suggest Burnside," said Mitzi. "The crew is expected to be in town all day, but time constraints may still be an issue. I'll be in touch with the interviewer tomorrow morning and then you and I can plan to get together again tomorrow afternoon, after I get more information. Thanks so much for suggesting this, Fred. You will be a wonderful representative for Bethlehem, and for the Society, as always."

"You are too kind," said Fred warmly. "Try to stay off that ankle. Get Vaughn to do the cooking tonight so you can rest. Take care, and I will see you tomorrow afternoon." Turning back again he asked, "Oh, and who were you thinking of as the female docent?"

"I might just have the perfect person in mind," answered Mitzi with a smile. "If I can track her down."

As Mitzi and Fred were meeting, Adele's meeting was in progress in the Church office conference room. The Communications Committee was very much a working committee of the Church responsible for the website, as well as for information about the ongoing outreach of the Church in the community. More than just a publicity committee, the Communications Committee promoted the Church's active social concern ministry in Bethlehem.

Adele was well aware that several of the members of the group also volunteered at Church-affiliated ministries in town, including the overnight shelter and Hospitality House, a place where anyone in need could come and enjoy a hot lunch each weekday. Some were tutors for the children who came to the drop-in center at the Spanish speaking outreach ministry on the City's south side.

Even before Adele could get the words out, one of the committee members said, "I hope that the camera crew coming to town next week will focus on some of the social concerns that we are dealing with as a community. The shelter, the food bank, Hospitality House, the drop-in center...these are all programs that should be emphasized in any promotional footage about the City of Bethlehem. Our history is important, of course, but we want people to know that we care about the people and the issues that we face today."

"Along those lines," said another committee member, "I would like to see something about specific social action initiatives of Central Church through the years - how the clothing boutique was started, for example, and how it is continuing today."

"Great ideas, thank you. You do realize that the final product will probably be a relatively short segment on the evening news, right?" asked Adele. "Mitzi and the Historical Society were the ones who were approached by the television network initially, so I am sure that they have ideas about the content of the segment, as well. But I will certainly pass on our comments from this meeting."

"Speaking of history though," said another committee member, "have you heard about one of the docents that the Society hired this year? I've never met her myself, but my daughter's Brownie troop raved about her. They said she was a really good storyteller on their walking tour and just a very nice person. They said it was like she was living in Bethlehem herself back in the 1700's. Apparently she stayed in character the whole time. They said it was odd, though, that she had the hood of her cape over her head, so you couldn't see her face that well."

"I've heard about her, too, but I haven't met her. After this woman docent helped Mitzi after her fall, I know that *Mitzi* is trying to find out who she is, too," said Adele. "At the moment she is a mystery lady, and a Good Samaritan at that."

CHAPTER FIVE

Spirits of Christmas Past

ADELE arrived at her office bright and early the next day, energized as she thought about the outreach discussion at yesterday's meeting. She decided to take a look at a few of the Church's old journals, which could be thought of as volumes of the modern day "Bethlehem Diary." She was hoping to find entries about the designation of Christmas Eve offerings for benevolent causes throughout the years. The journals were mostly handwritten by the pastors of the time, so they were sometimes a challenge to decipher.

She found three specific causes that were highlighted on half-page inserts in the church programs. One was a plea for contributions toward hurricane relief in Jamaica. Another was for help in building a parsonage for a new church start in California; another for hurricane relief in Tobago, an island near Trinidad.

Of course, Central Church itself was in need of help in November of 1941, when fire broke out in the building, the day before the installation of the Church's new pastor. There was damage to the organ and to the sanctuary itself, which had just been refurbished and newly painted. The funds it would cost to restore the building seemed modest by today's standards, but back then, $50,000 was a huge amount of money. According to newspaper articles that were pasted into the journal, many of the community's churches stepped forward to offer their facilities to Central for worship. Because Central could use its own Old Chapel and Christian Education Building for worship, the Church didn't need to accept the invitations, although the many gestures of kindness were much appreciated.

Thinking that she would mention some of these stories of Advent and Christmases past in her sermon, she re-shelved the old journals, promising herself to get back to them and do more reading, one of these days. Then she turned to her file cabinet, pulled out a folder marked "Christmas Eve" and sat down at her desk. Over the years, she had saved all of the prayers that she offered during the services. As she flipped through the prayers tucked inside each of the programs, she looked at the dates that she had written on the corner of each page. "Christmas Eve 1984" was her first Christmas at the Church. She remembered how amazing and magical it had seemed back then, when she was an associate pastor, before she really understood all that was involved in preparing for 3 services on that one day involving at least 3,000 congregants and visitors, sacristans, fire watchers, collectors, choir members and musicians. She had come to appreciate the services even more now, after learning so much more about the months of preparations that went into those few hours each Christmas Eve.

The prayer for "Christmas 2001" was an especially poignant one, of course. At that time, people were still in pain over the loss of lives on September 11, and still apprehensive about the direction that the country would take in response to the attacks, yet depending on their faith to sustain them.

Each Christmas in Bethlehem was memorable in its own way, some with those panicked moments that you'd like to forget. She thought about the time that a cookie order for the Children's Lovefeast was short and the Head Sacrist had to go out to any store that he could find open, in search of 20 dozen sugar cookies! Then there was the year, well before she came to the Church, that a great snowstorm the day before had forced the sacristans to take rooms at the Hotel overnight, just so they could walk across the street and get to the services on Christmas Eve on time.

Well, things were going to go smoothly this year, Adele thought confidently. All would be well. She would just quickly run up to the office attic to pick up another copy of the Children's Lovefeast ode, the program of hymns and anthems for Christmas Eve. Then she would be on her way to do some hospital visitation. But after searching all of the shelves and boxes where service materials were stored, there were no odes to be found in the attic.

She went downstairs and checked in with the Church Secretary, Margaret. "Have you stored the odes somewhere else?" she asked. "I couldn't find the box."

"If they aren't up there, they are probably in the Church. Let me check. I'm sure they are around, in fact I remember thinking how many extra copies we had."

"Thanks," Adele said on her way out the door. "I'll be back before noon to pick up a copy."

But when she arrived back at the office after her hospital visits, Margaret reported that no one could find the odes. Anywhere. At all. Adele pulled out her key to the Church and said, "I'll take a look. Maybe they're in the Vestry closet." She wasn't worried just yet. After all, how could you lose 1,000 odes? And they were printed on lime green paper, for Pete's sake. You couldn't possibly miss them.

An hour later, she enlisted the help of the music director, Scott, and Ellen, the organist, and Bill, an unsuspecting board member who happened to drop by to say "hello," but still no odes. Adele finally went up to the choir loft herself and sat in a side pew for a moment to ponder where the odes might possibly be. The organist, having tired of the search, sat down at the organ and had begun to practice for this Sunday.

Just then, Adele felt a bump on the back of her pew. Odd. It was strong enough to push her forward a bit, so she looked behind her to see if someone had come up to the balcony and sat down behind her and tried to get her attention. No one was there. I must be losing it, she thought. I'm imagining things. And then it happened again, this time harder. Again, she looked around and saw no one, just the organist playing at the front of the balcony and the empty sanctuary below.

Adele stood up quickly this time, a bit spooked by what had happened. As she turned and started up the steps to the stairwell, there in the corner she saw a large cardboard box wedged between two storage cabinets. Taped to the outside of the box was the lime green program. You've got to be kidding, she thought. Did someone just show me where the odes were?

"Ellen," she called out. "Here are the odes. Did you happen to see anyone come in while you were playing? "

The organist stopped playing, smiled and shook her head. "This wouldn't be the first time that I've felt that someone was up here. I always think of Mr. Brantley and how much he loved to sit in the balcony on Christmas Eve. Maybe he wanted to help you out," she said, shrugging her shoulders and starting to play again.

Mr. Brantley, of course, had passed away on Christmas Eve about five years ago. He had arrived early for the service, as usual, and was suddenly taken ill. A paramedic in the choir called an ambulance, but he died on the way to the hospital.

Adele was really not one to believe in ghosts, but some of her colleagues were. The Church Sexton, for example. He swore that he was alone in the sanctuary one evening and as he turned off the last of the lights in the building, the organ began to play - all by itself. Adele made a mental note not to mention to the Sexton how she found the box of odes. All kinds of stories made the rounds through the years, of course, like the one about the time a woman who was sitting in the Old Chapel looked up at the high windows in the darkened, empty Church, right across the alley. There in the window of the second floor Kleiner Saal, she saw very clearly the face of a woman dressed in colonial garb.

So were these stories all just fiction, figments of active imaginations? At this point in a busy season, I'm not even going to try to figure it out, thought Adele, as she pushed the box of odes over to the landing for the Sexton to retrieve later. She doubted that good old Mr. Brantley would be kind enough to carry the odes downstairs.

CHAPTER SIX

Bethlehem Histories

WORKING and living in Bethlehem was always inspiring, often intriguing, and sometimes even downright exciting, thought Mitzi. The rich history of the Moravians was around every corner. The history of the great steel company that once defined the town was apparent too, especially on the city's south side. Along with the history of industry, beginning in colonial days, were fascinating individual histories of each one of the immigrant workers and their families who came to this country and forged the modern community. There were great stories to tell, and she enjoyed every opportunity to tell them.

Undeniably, though, the Advent and Christmas seasons in Bethlehem, for her and for the Historical Society, were the most hectic and challenging times of the year.

As the Christmas City, Bethlehem welcomed tourists from all around the country and the world. Mitzi was often called upon to give small private tours to visiting dignitaries of local businesses and of the Moravian Church worldwide. But the day-to-day hospitality for these few packed weeks was extended primarily to people on bus tours to the area. Overall, everything worked remarkably smoothly, when you considered that each bus contained 50 plus people and their guides who were on tight schedules as they visited the museums, gift shops and Christmas Putz within the historic district.

Times were beginning to change, though, and the once predictable and constrained itinerary of a typical bus tour could now get derailed mid-stream. After waiting for an hour for a bus to arrive one evening, for example, Mitzi's tour coordinator discovered that the group of out-of-towners on the bus decided to skip the downtown sights in favor of a trip to a nearby shopping mall!

People did like to shop, of course. The Society's Visitor Center itself contained a wonderful gift shop. It featured handcrafted items from local artisans and businesses. It carried everything from note cards to iron door handles made at the Smithy. Handmade candles, folded paper stars, jewelry, colorful knit items and wall hangings filled the space. Mitzi's staff members were well informed about the tours that visitors could take, as well as about times and venues for other events in the area. People were appreciative, too, thought Mitzi. So many visitors returned year after year and stopped in to say "hello," as part of their nostalgic journey home.

The more she thought about hospitality, the more she wondered how to identify and then how to find the elusive costumed guide, whom she now thought of as the Mystery Docent. All that Mitzi knew was that the docent was rather tall and slender, was very knowledgeable about Bethlehem and seemed to relate well to children and adults alike. On that day on the Green when Mitzi fell and hurt her ankle, she was too busy trying to stand up, and the mystery lady disappeared so quickly that Mitzi herself couldn't recollect any further details about the woman.

Mitzi had to find her before the filming, but how? Fred just might have to do a solo presentation, if she failed.

CHAPTER SEVEN

'Tis the Season

ADELE turned the distinctive brass scroll-in-hand door pull as she put the key in the Church door lock for the umpteenth time that day. Then she set the latch so that the door would remain open for the next group of musicians to come in to rehearse. She was on her way home for the evening, but told the Sexton that she would stop by the church and open the door herself; he needn't stay.

She walked down the hall toward the northeast door and opened the electrical box on the wall, flipped on the pulpit lights and spots and double-checked to see if the large Moravian star overhead in the sanctuary was lighted. On the first Sunday of Advent, the star was hung in the apse, in the front of the sanctuary. Later, when the front of the Church was decorated, it would be moved to the back of the sanctuary to remain there for the rest of the season. Within the apse, the sacristans of the church would put in place a large nativity scene painted on canvas. Undecorated, live evergreens flanked the painting, which was surrounded by handmade rock cloth and real straw.

The controls for the distinctive cove lights all around the large sanctuary, just under the curve of the ceiling, were back in the West Rooms, on the other end of the building. She made her way down the aisle, glancing at the pew racks to see if all of the brochures were resupplied. Just then, she heard a creaking sound coming from the back hallway. "CJ, is that you?" she called out, thinking that the Sexton had stopped by anyway. There was no reply. Probably just the normal sounds of the old building at night, she thought. This poor sanctuary gets put through its paces, she mused, moving on to the West Rooms. No wonder it sounds so creaky at times.

Her predecessor, Baxter had been absolutely right, she had to admit. Keeping the Church calendar straight was probably the biggest challenge for a pastor of the largest downtown Moravian Church, especially during the Advent and Christmas seasons, beginning in mid-November through the first week of January. Over that time period, hundreds of daytime and evening events were scheduled for the Church sanctuary, the Old Chapel and the Christian Education Building.

The nearby college made use of Central Church for its Christmas Vespers, which meant that rehearsal times for their various groups and musicians had to be factored in, as well. A series of community programs called "An Old Fashioned Moravian Christmas" was a draw for visitors and members alike, but those programs added their own time and space demands to the already packed schedule. Mini-concerts were miraculously shoehorned into any time slots that remained. Adele remembered with horror the afternoon when all of the groups seemed to collide as concerned looking brass players and determined, white-gloved bell choir ringers faced off in front of the pulpit, each staking a claim on the sanctuary for a rehearsal. The Christmas spirit prevailed, to Adele's surprise and relief, and some quick negotiating made it work for everyone.

Although the Christian Education Building was a smaller venue, the Putz caused its share of traffic jams among walk-in visitors and tour bus riders. You had to keep your sense of humor, thought Adele, as she recalled the sight of a wild-eyed tour bus director wearing a ridiculous set of reindeer antlers, arriving at the back door of the building, guiding her flock of Jewish ladies and asking forlornly, "Is this where we're supposed to be?"

Christmas in Bethlehem meant Christmas with visitors. There was no doubt about it. Nor was there any doubt that members of her congregation were always more than happy to welcome people and to give them an overview of Moravian history and even a tour of the campus. A few years back, one of the Putz volunteers shepherded a man around the campus who turned out to be a writer for a large New York City newspaper. The feature story the following weekend was how Christmas in Bethlehem was, well, somewhat surprisingly, mostly about Christmas.

Not that Bethlehem merchants weren't prepared for the onslaught of tourists. Stores along Main Street were filled to overflowing with their wares, storefronts shone brightly with Moravian stars and the bare trees in front of the stores were decked with tiny white lights. As a child, Adele could remember the much less tasteful decorations of the fifties with their gaudy, brightly colored tinsel-covered ornaments strung across the streets. It was a spectacle back then, to be sure, and much nicer now, she thought. Although when she thought of how it used to be, she thought wistfully about her grandfather taking her and her grandmother on magical, leisurely drives down Main Street at night.

As an adult, and as a pastor, just beneath the panic and stress of the season was always the nostalgia that came along with Christmas in Bethlehem. She hoped that it would never change. But she also hoped that Bethlehem would continue to be the Christmas City in its best sense. A spirit of love, a spirit of hospitality and welcome; these were the essentials of the Christmas City.

As she walked down the aisle of the sanctuary that evening, toward the door leading to Church Street, she thought for a moment that her eyes were playing tricks on her. Someone crossed quickly and silently from the door to the east hallway. She hadn't heard the massive old door swing open, had she? It wasn't unusual to see people coming and going at all hours, so she was not overly concerned.

"Hello? May I help you?" she called out. No answer. The sound of a book falling from the shelf in the vestry made her curious. "Chaplain, is that you?" she called out again. "I was just..." She stopped mid-sentence as she saw the grey skirts of a docent swing around the corner into the adjacent sacristy. Wondering if this could be the "mystery" docent, she hurriedly followed, chattering away, "Hold up a moment, please. Are you the one who helped my friend Mitzi the other day?"

But as she stepped into the sacristy, no one was there. For just a moment, a chill ran down Adele's back as she realized that either she was seeing things, or her Mystery Docent had once again just vanished into thin air.

CHAPTER EIGHT

"Mind the Carriage, Sir!"

SATURDAY lunch was generally the time when Adele and Zeke could catch up with each other and talk about what was happening in their hectic lives. During the week, Adele had at least three evening meetings and a late afternoon Bible study to teach. Zeke's schedule was almost as demanding, and his twice weekly basketball games were sacrosanct.

After checking in with each other on the latest neighborhood news, Adele began to regale Zeke with the story of the "Mystery Docent," and the woman's sudden appearance and then disappearance at Church the day before.

"Maybe it was someone from the College," said Zeke. "Aren't they in the sanctuary a lot these days?"

"Maybe," said Adele, "but whoever it was could have at least identified themselves."

"And Mitzi doesn't know who she might be?"

"Not a clue. It would be very unlikely that Mitzi wouldn't have met her somewhere along the way."

"Did Mitzi talk to her treasurer? If this Mystery Docent were a new hire, he would at least have had her fill out a W-4."

"Good point," agreed Adele. "I should mention that to Mitzi."

"Did I tell you that I got stopped by a docent this morning? My ball game on Sand Island was cancelled at the last minute, so I decided to take a run up the hill and around a couple of blocks downtown, just for some exercise. I was crossing Church Street down by Main, running with my head down, as usual. Just then I hear this woman yelling, 'Mind the carriage, sir!' I looked up and stopped just in time before the horse and carriage came by."

"You could have been run over! Those carriage horses may not be fast, but they certainly are big! So you're telling me that the Mystery Docent struck again?"

"And you're sure that it wasn't Sally? That's who I suspected that the mystery lady might be."

"It wasn't Sally. I think I just saw Sally a minute or two before, over in front of the Single Brethren's House. She and her husband waved to me on their way up to the Church office, or at least it looked like them."

"Huh. Then this really is a mystery. With everything going on right now, maybe we'll just have to wait till after Christmas to figure it all out."

CHAPTER NINE

Dinner at the Shelter

THE local shelter for homeless men was started a number of years ago by the downtown Bethlehem churches. At the beginning of the ministry, each church hosted the shelter on a rotating basis in its own fellowship hall, bringing in cots for sleeping and comfortable furniture for a living room area. With the help of church volunteers, the shelter worked as well as could be expected in makeshift surroundings. But it became evident that a better solution needed to be found.

Adele sat on the original board for the shelter and was pleased that the transition from a month to month shelter to a permanent location had been successful. Many of the members of Central Church remained steadfast volunteers at the shelter throughout the years. Not only could the homeless guests find a safe and comfortable place to stay overnight, they were also offered job training and help with finding a permanent place to live. When new members were received into the Church, the pastors always presented opportunities for individuals to get involved in volunteering at the shelter, as well as in a host of other community programs.

At Adele's suggestion, Pastor Sally and her husband Chris decided to get some hands-on experience and help out at the shelter at dinner time. This particular afternoon, just as Sally and Chris were walking across the parking lot from their car, they encountered Mark Sargent and Beth Ettwein. "On duty this evening?" asked Beth, smiling and extending her hand.

"Yes we are," said Chris, introducing himself and Sally. "We're new to this, so I hope you can show us the ropes."

"No problem," said Mark, shaking hands. "We both like to cook, so it's fun for us."

"What's on the menu this evening?" asked Sally.

"We don't usually know in advance what supplies are available, but people have been very generous with their donations. We can usually create something really nice," chimed in Beth.

They stepped into the large, bright kitchen and within a few moments, made plans for the evening meal and divided up the prep work, the cooking and serving. The men who came to dinner were as appreciative as always and pitched in with the cleanup afterward.

The evening went by quickly, as the two young couples shared a bit about themselves as they worked.

Sally and Chris were fascinated to hear Beth and Mark talk about their search for an old historic home in town to purchase and renovate together. Although the Church had found a great apartment for Sally and Chris, they always dreamed of having a home of their own, too.

"We've been looking at a property on High Street," said Beth, as they turned off the kitchen lights and began to leave. "It's actually an old home that my mom owns. I think that she might be willing to negotiate a good price."

"Elaine was smart to buy that property years ago. It is right inside the historic district and has a lot of potential as a family home, with a rental apartment attached to it," said Mark.

"We would love to see it sometime, if we could," said Sally. Chris nodded, "We're looking to buy a home, eventually. It would be good to get to know the neighborhood."

"If you guys are free this Saturday morning, we'd love for you to come over and see the house. Say about 9:30?" asked Beth.

Saturday morning was unseasonably warm for December as the two couples walked around the perimeter of the home on High Street, admiring the landscaping that Beth's mother Elaine herself had undertaken last fall with her new husband Merrill. Beth was as surprised as anyone in town when Elaine and Merrill announced their engagement last summer. Elaine's first husband, Beth's father, was a wonderful man with a gregarious personality who passed away several years ago. Merrill, for as long as anyone remembered, was a kind of curmudgeon - that is, until he met Elaine. Who would have thought, pondered Beth. Merrill couldn't be a better partner for her mother. Plus, he was a gardening enthusiast who really worked hard at making the property they were looking at today a showplace.

"It's actually getting kind of warm out here," said Mark, wiping his brow as they stood in the fenced in yard. "Let's take a look inside."

The interior of the home needed some updating, but it was still obvious that the place was a treasure. Mark and Beth showed Chris and Sally the first floor and then led the way upstairs to the second and third floors. Each of the four bedrooms was spacious and sunny, two with cozy window seats and all of the rooms revealing charming touches that made the home especially appealing.

As Mark opened the door to the attic, he cautioned, "This is the space that needs the most work, but I think it would be worth it to renovate."

Sally and Chris could not believe what a huge expanse the attic occupied, stretching clear across the house as one large room. Although some of the walls were added more recently and dry walled, some still revealed the original wallpaper over the old lath and plaster construction.

"If walls could talk, eh?" said Chris. "I'll bet that this house could tell lots of stories. I've always been fascinated by what people find when they begin to renovate."

"We'll find out soon enough," smiled Mark. "Beth and I just talked with Beth's mom, and the house is officially ours! Next comes the renovation."

"And the wedding!" said Beth. "Sounds easy enough doesn't it? Plan a wedding and renovate a house at the same time?"

Sally and Chris congratulated the couple and insisted that they needed a celebratory lunch, plus the promise of help with the renovation. As Mark closed the attic door firmly behind them, and continued laughing and talking, none of them could hear the faint scraping sound of a small package wrapped in newspaper slipping down the inside of the wall.

CHAPTER TEN

Clues at the Burnside Plantation

HER friend Fred Lang was right, Mitzi thought, it was a good idea to have the television crew include the Burnside Plantation in its taping. She decided that it would be wise to spend some time at the property, to check out some possible locations to suggest. You tended to look at a place differently, too, when you thought about sharing it with others.

Taking advantage of the unseasonably warm December afternoon, Mitzi convinced Vaughn to join her on her mission. Turning in just off of Paint Mill Road, they parked their car at what had been the old corn crib. From there they walked the sloping grounds, now somewhat bare of vegetation during winter, but still lovely.

Vaughn enjoyed Burnside as much as Mitzi, volunteering to help with the Blueberry Festival that was held there each July, as well as pitching in with the decorating of the buildings on the property each Christmas season. In this tranquil space not far from the heart of the city, he could easily imagine what life would have been like on a colonial farm. The hundreds of acres of fields that would have been part of the plantation were sold off long ago, of course, but what remained allowed visitors to catch a glimpse of everyday life in Bethlehem in the colonial era.

The main house of the Plantation was a two story stone building set on a gentle hill. Part of the home was still the original structure built by James Burnside; the other portion was an extension added in the early 1800's. The house looked out onto the large garden where volunteers transformed the open stretch of land each summer, planting and harvesting vegetables and flowers.

Mitzi unlocked the old front door, while Vaughn righted the large grapevine wreath, hanging slightly askew on the side of the house. They felt like they were coming home, since they had both invested many hours of work alongside the Society's volunteers in deciding how to choose and display furniture and artifacts that would have been typical of the time.

James Burnside was the first owner of private property in the old Moravian community, purchasing 500 acres of land to the north of the heart of the settlement. He was a native of Ireland, but had come to live and work with the Moravians in their earlier settlement in Georgia. After his first wife died, Burnside traveled to Bethlehem and purchased this property. His young daughter, who was living and going to school in Nazareth, died tragically of smallpox. Burnside then met and married a widow from New York, Mary Wendover, and brought her to Bethlehem.

More suited to the political life than farming, Burnside became a member of the first Provincial Assembly and worked beside Benjamin Franklin and others to assure that the rights of Pennsylvania landowners were respected.

After Burnside died, within a few years, his widow, Mary, returned to New York and subsequently left the land and buildings to the Moravian Church. The Church eventually sold the property to another Moravian, Charles Luckenbach. Through the years, different private owners acquired the property; some of the owners dividing portions of it for sale. In the late 1980's the property came into the hands of what was to become Bethlehem's Historical Society.

Not a great deal was known about Mary Wendover Burnside, except that she and James never had children of their own. And, as volunteers discovered in doing some research online, Mary was the first to contribute 50 dollars toward the building of the Widows' House on Church Street near Central Church.

Mitzi often thought that if Mary were alive today, she might be pleased with how beautifully her home here at the Plantation had been restored and kept.

"What's this?" Vaughn asked, bringing Mitzi out of her reverie. He picked up an apron and haube that were neatly folded and sitting on a chair in the kitchen. "Should these be put away?"

"Maybe one of the docents left them out," said Mitzi. "Let me take a look." Unfolding the long, white apron, quite soft from years of use, she noticed that on the inside, near the turn of the hem, someone had embroidered the initials, "MWB."

"This looks like an original garment," she said, examining the apron more closely, and then the haube. The haube had ties of white ribbon, indicating that the wearer would have been a widow. "These should be packed in tissue and stored properly. I wonder who would have left them just sitting out on a chair?"

Deciding to tuck the items into a drawer for temporary safekeeping, Mitzi made a mental note to call her curator to come and pick them up for storage in their climate-controlled space in a different building.

"I wonder if someone has been using the house as a changing area," said Vaughn. "There is a mug in the sink, and one of the cupboard doors is open."

Mitzi could come up with no explanation for what she saw. Docents were asked to change at the Museum on Church Street. And certainly, none of them would have access to the Burnside home without permission.

"Maybe we have ghosts," grinned Vaughn. "At least they're from the right era!"

"I think I need to ask my staff some questions," Mitzi said. "I might have to do a little detective work. Let's put things in order so that the camera crew can get right to their filming next week, if they choose to film inside."

For the next few minutes, Vaughn and Mitzi straightened up the kitchen and then took a brief look around the rest of the building, making sure that everything was secure. They locked the door, set the alarm and walked away from the house just as the sun was setting over the tall trees that bordered the meadow. The sky was so brilliantly beautiful that evening that they did not notice the flicker of a single candle in the kitchen window of the old Burnside home.

CHAPTER ELEVEN

Treasure in the Walls

AT their newly acquired home on High Street, Mark and Beth worked all morning to make a list of renovations that they wanted to try to tackle before they moved in. Some of the carpentry would be done by friends of Beth's mother who had offered their help. Plumbing and electrical work would be contracted out to two local companies. The decorating, including painting and wallpapering, would be done by Mark and Beth themselves, with the assistance of their friends Sally and Chris.

Each room had its challenges, so the list of items to do grew longer and longer. In some cases, the young couple was torn with the question of how much to change and how much to try to restore. The sun room on the first floor was perfect for a nursery someday, for example, but it would need heating and the replacement of all of the big old windows that enclosed it.

When the couple finally made it up the stairs to the attic, they wondered just how much of that space they could afford to remodel. Maybe drywall and electrical outlets would be all they could put in their budget for now. Still, the space was so appealing, they hoped that they could do more.

"Let's take a break for a minute, shall we?' asked Beth. She pulled up an old bench and pointed Mark to a wicker chair stacked with magazines.

"I'm ready for a break," said Mark, clearing the magazines and pulling his chair over to Beth. "Maybe we should take another look at this list and see if we can eliminate some items. I would really like to get this attic space renovated. There is a lot we could do with it."

"Well," said Beth, flipping through two pages of notes, "this is what we have so far. I'm not sure what we could cut."

As they talked over the projects that were needed, they watched how the light made its way around the substantial attic windows and how the tall trees created a dappled shade from the sun. "This is really beautiful up here in the afternoon, isn't it?" asked Mark. "Maybe it is a little unorthodox, but wouldn't this make a great second living room space?"

"Or maybe a master bedroom plus sitting area," said Beth. "And the downstairs room that would have been the master could be our guest room and putz room."

"Then all we would need is a putz!" said Mark, smiling.

"We know a lot of Moravians in Bethlehem," said Beth, laughing. "Somebody we know could certainly give us a hand with a putz!"

"So let's think about making this the master bedroom," said Mark, getting up from his chair and starting to tap the walls to determine if they were dealing with wallboard or plaster. "The electrical work would probably be the biggest issue. Vents for heating would have to be installed." Just then, they heard a soft, but distinct thud behind the wall that Mark was tapping.

"What was that?" Beth said, jumping up from her seat. "I wonder if it is a dead animal or something."

"Let's find out," said Mark. "This wallboard is loose and it looks like it would need to be replaced anyway."

"Okay, but I'm not dealing with any dead critters," said Beth, taking a step back.

Mark found an iron lamp base to use as a hammer and began knocking it gently against the wallboard close to the floor. The corner of the board gave way easily and crumbled in his grasp. There, behind the wall, was what looked like a small package wrapped tightly in newspaper. It had apparently fallen down the track created by the wooden studs.

"This is interesting," said Mark. "At least it isn't a dead squirrel."

Beth made a face as she stooped down next to Mark. "What is it?"

"It's kind of wedged in here," said Mark, tugging at the package. Finally he dislodged it, tearing the newspaper in the process. Poking out of the brittle old paper was what looked like the foot of a figurine.

Mark carefully unwrapped the rest of the package, setting aside the newspaper to look at later. "I think it is a figurine, like people use in a putz," he said, turning it around to inspect it. "Doesn't it kind of look like one of the Wise Men? He's got a treasure chest in his hands."

"It does," said Beth. "I'll bet it was used in a putz! Our first figure for our own putz!"

"This thing certainly has some weight to it." said Mark. "Here, hold this," he said, handing the brightly painted figure to Beth.

"But that's good, isn't it," she said. "You won't be able to knock it over."

"Let's look at the date of the newspaper," said Mark, smoothing a page out on the bench. "It says, "November 12, 1947.""

"I wonder who owned the house back then? That would be post World War II, right before the Advent season," said Beth. "Maybe Mom would know. I'm curious now to see if there are any other pieces hidden away in the walls."

"We have our answer then, don't we?" asked Mark. "The walls come down and get replaced!"

"And we start planning our putz for the downstairs room," said Beth, holding up the Wise Man. "Let's see if we can pull together a putz for this season. Then we can have an open house to show it off, and recruit more of our friends to help out with the remodeling!"

"You are a conniving woman, Beth Ettwein," said Mark, laughing and hugging her close. "That's what I love about you."

CHAPTER TWELVE

Just Another Evening in Bethlehem

THE day of the taping for the network arrived, and Mitzi was still not able to identify the elusive docent who continued to get such rave reviews from tourists and townspeople alike. It really was a mystery, Mitzi thought, as she stacked some of the paperwork that had been accumulating on her desk for her assistant to file. Time was running out, so Mitzi needed to make a decision about whom to call. It would have to be someone who was available on very short notice.

"Adele on line 1," said her assistant through the intercom. "She has a suggestion for you."

"Thanks Amy. I hope she has a docent in mind for this evening."

Amy connected the call, but even before Mitzi had a chance to say hello, Adele said, "Your worries are over, Mitzi! I know who the Mystery Docent is!"

"I wish that all of my worries were over," said Mitzi. "Who is the mystery woman?"

"It's Sally! My Sally at Central! Well, at least I think so," said Adele, "even though Zeke says it couldn't possibly be Sally."

"How did you figure that out?" asked Mitzi, genuinely surprised. "Did she confess?"

"Well, sort of. I found a colonial costume hanging inside her office, and when I asked her about it, she was pretty sheepish about the whole thing."

"Would she be ready to talk to the TV interviewer this evening?"

"Way ahead of you, Mitzi," said Adele, "She will meet us at Church and Main Streets at 5:30 pm. She won't be able to join you and Fred at Burnside though, but I told her that I thought that would be okay."

"Actually, that would be fine," Mitzi agreed. "Fred and I can handle the Burnside segment and then we'll meet you both later."

"Told you we would solve the mystery," chirped Adele. "I think we should even write up the "Sally story" for our newsletters! It might be a fun, human interest piece."

"That's a good idea. But first let's get through this evening. See you soon."

That afternoon, Fred had his opportunity to accompany the crew to Burnside, where he and Mitzi were able to help set up some locations for filming. They wanted to focus primarily on the grounds and exterior of the buildings.

Mitzi turned off the security alarm and opened the Burnside home for the crew members, who needed a place to warm up for a few minutes before moving on. As she walked into the kitchen, a distinct chill crept up her spine as she saw the long white apron and haube sitting on a chair. How did they get here, she wondered as she looked over at the drawer in the dresser where she had put them just yesterday. Did they belong to Sally, if she were the Mystery Docent? How would she have gotten in the house? Mitzi stood staring at the apron for a moment, not knowing what to make of what she saw. She would have to ask Sally what was going on, but for now she had to lock up the Burnside home and move on to Church and Main.

All that she would remember from this evening would be the chaos of it, thought Adele, as she hurried along Main Street with the TV network film crew. Her friend Mitzi was a bit more accustomed to dealing with the quick, almost frantic pace of a television crew and interviewer on a mission.

First, there had been the late arrival of the TV people for this segment of the filming. Mitzi and Adele, Fred and Sally had stood in the cold at the corner of Church and Main Streets for well over 30 minutes, waiting to greet the network vehicles and direct them into the Hotel parking lot.

When everyone was finally situated and lights and microphones were in place, the interviewer, Megan Kaplan immediately and totally off script, turned her attention to the lighted star on South Mountain.

"Tell us something about the star and how it got there," said Megan to Mitzi, who was much more eager to introduce her two costumed docents who stood shivering nearby. Fred actually seemed fine, but Sally looked frozen. She was trying unsuccessfully to conceal the fuzzy white mittens that she was wearing under the voluminous folds of her cape.

After filming the distant star for what seemed to be a good five minutes, Megan decided to have the crew face Main Street, looking north. "The lights outside the shops are so beautiful, " she said. "How are the merchants feeling about this Christmas season? Are sales up or down? What's the economy like in the area?"

Mitzi did her best to field the questions, but she was determined to move on to more of the historical information that she and Fred had planned to share. Fred, as usual, was his bright-eyed, upbeat self, not noticing or caring how cold it was to be standing on a windy corner on a December evening. Sally was smiling, but now and then looked longingly into the cozy, warm Book Shop nearby.

Much to everyone's surprise, the interview and the filming went very well, with Fred and Sally staying in character, describing their own 18th century Moravian Bethlehem and Mitzi and Adele filling in with facts, figures and anecdotes on the more contemporary aspects of the city. Adele was especially pleased to share some of the work of local churches in providing food, clothing and shelter to those in need. Megan seemed very satisfied with what they were able to cover, as well. As she said her final goodbyes, she promised to come back again next year.

Fred's wife Doris and Sally's husband Chris appeared quickly to retrieve their spouses. Mitzi and Adele lingered a bit, stopping for a few moments near the long, curved brownstone steps of Central Church to reflect on the filming. It had started to snow and the sidewalks and trees were quickly turning white. The town could not have been more beautiful.

Mitzi was just about to tell Adele about the apron and haube that she found at Burnside that afternoon, when a horse and carriage made its way around the corner onto Main Street at a rather fast pace for a regular city tour.

They looked over at the open carriage and saw that a middle-aged woman who was sitting in the carriage seemed to be leaning back and moaning in great distress. The anxious man sitting next to her was trying to calm her, but he was looking right and left, as if he were trying to find help.

"She's pregnant," said Adele, "and she sounds like she might be in labor!"

"Let's go see if we can help," said Mitzi, already on the phone, calling an ambulance.

The two women hurried toward the carriage as it pulled up next to the Book Shop, near the Christmas booths.

"I've called an ambulance for you," Mitzi said, opening the low door to the open carriage. "They should be here soon."

"Looks like the baby might get here before they do," said the distraught husband, helping his wife step down out of the carriage onto the brick sidewalk.

"Maybe we should get her into this booth at the corner," said Adele. "She needs to be under cover and lie down."

Although the market had closed for the evening, there were still some vendors moving their merchandise inside and shuttering the fronts of their booths. The vendor closest to the carriage stop motioned them over.

Trying to act as normally as possible for his wife's sake the man said, "I'm Joe, and this is my wife, Irene."

"This will be my fourth," said Irene, gritting her teeth between contractions. "He's just about ready to make an appearance!"

Adele and Joe helped his wife hobble the few steps to the booth as the vendor spread out some blankets on the narrow floor.

As Adele stepped back, she heard a familiar voice behind her. "Adele, what's going on? I came out of the Book Shop and saw you rushing in this direction." It was her niece, Karen, a nurse, out for an evening of Christmas shopping while her husband watched the kids. Karen had two children, the baby just 9 months old. Thank goodness, Adele thought. A recent veteran!

Between Karen and Mitzi, who actually had some emergency medical training, the mom-to-be was in good hands. All she needed to do was to stay calm until the ambulance arrived. Adele stood at the doorway, transfixed. Joe anxiously stood watch for the ambulance, pacing back and forth in front of the booth, but it was certainly taking them a long time to get there. Adele stepped out of the booth to pace with Joe for a moment.

Then suddenly, they all heard the small, but strong and healthy wail of a newborn, just as the ambulance arrived with lights flashing and siren sounding. It was quite an entrance that this child had made.

Karen and Mitzi had done a fantastic job as volunteer midwives, and little Jonathan was born into the world, safe and sound. His mom smiled as they wrapped him in one of the soft shawls the vendor offered. "An early Christmas gift," he said.

"This was one unbelievable evening," said Adele, as she and Mitzi watched the ambulance pull away. "Dealing with TV crews and delivering babies. Is there anything you can't do?" she asked teasingly.

"Vaughn is never going to believe this, that's for sure. By the way, why was the ambulance so slow in getting here tonight? They are usually so quick to respond."

"You won't believe this either," said Adele, "They were held up because our film crew vehicle had a fender bender right in front of them! They told me that everyone is okay, but that they couldn't get through for a good ten minutes or so."

"Did the film crew know that they missed out on the story of the season?" asked Mitzi.

Adele smiled as she imagined the network tagline, the words fitting in so beautifully with the season: "Another Christmas miracle: Baby born in wooden stall in Bethlehem."

CHAPTER THIRTEEN

Still a Mystery

THE next morning, Adele arrived at the Church office early and started the coffee and set out the bagels for the weekly staff meeting. Regardless of TV interviews or even delivering babies, Church life went on, and with more exciting events to come, no doubt.

Adele heard the back door open and saw Sally peek her head around the corner of the workroom. "Good morning," she said, "Were you pleased with last evening?"

"Do you mean the filming or the delivery of the baby?" laughed Adele, as she told a wide-eyed Sally what had happened after she went home.

"I thought that this was a quiet little town," said Sally, shaking her head.

"It is, for the most part. Things just get a tiny bit interesting at Christmas time. To be honest with you, I thought that our big hoopla this year was going to be the Mystery Docent."

"Mystery Docent?" asked Sally. "Who is that?"

"Come on, Sally! *You* are, of course," said Adele. "I figured it out when I saw your Moravian costume hanging in your office. You were the one who was helping out with the tours and getting such good reviews!"

"Adele, I really don't know what you're talking about," said Sally slowly. "I borrowed the outfit for a program at a luncheon that the Busy Workers are having next week. They want me to be the Countess Benigna, Count Zinzendorf's daughter. I've never even tried on the costume."

"You're kidding," said Adele. "Do you mean to say that we still have a Mystery Docent on the loose?"

Although she didn't know it at the time, right outside the office window, an early morning group of a dozen tourists ambled by, led by a petite blonde costumed guide. At the end of the group, a tall guide wearing a full costume and haube with a white ribbon followed quietly along.

CHAPTER FOURTEEN

A Christmas Open House

IT was an odd phenomenon in Bethlehem that happened every year during the week before Christmas. There was a lull, no, maybe more of a brief slowdown, Adele thought. The Christmas Market had closed its doors for the season. The concerts in the sanctuary for the college and schools were all complete. Bus tours had dwindled to a near standstill so close to Christmas. The Putz was a bit quieter, as people stayed home or were more focused on doing their last minute shopping.

Mitzi, Adele and Sally managed to find time for lunch one day at the Hotel. Mitzi was glad to have the opportunity to get to know Sally a bit better, since they were together so briefly on the evening of the filming.

"How did your program for the Busy Workers go last week?" Mitzi asked Sally after they ordered.

"It was good," Sally said. "I had to do some research on Benigna, since I know that the ladies in Busy Workers know their Moravian history!"

"She did a great job," said Adele, as Sally smiled at the compliment. "I think we have a potential actress among us - she is just not the Mystery Docent!"

"I am still puzzled about who that docent might be," said Mitzi. "When you mentioned to me, Adele, that you thought it was Sally, I was somewhat relieved. It isn't every day that we come across someone who mysteriously pops up out of nowhere."

Sally laughed, "You thought it was me?"

"Just wait - you haven't heard this story yet," said Mitzi. "Vaughn and I discovered an apron and haube at the Burnside home before the filming. We thought it might belong to the Mystery Docent, but we couldn't quite make the connection. I tucked the apron and haube away myself, but the following day when we came back with the film crew, the two items were sitting out on the chair again."

"That's kind of spooky," said Adele. "Who could they belong to?"

"I hesitate to mention this," said Mitzi, "but the initials that were embroidered on the hem of the apron were "MWB.""

"They could stand for Mary Wendover Burnside, couldn't they?" asked Sally. "I came across the Burnside story when I was doing my research. I found out that Mary, even though she was originally from New York, was very fond of Bethlehem. She gave a contribution toward the building of the Widows' House and left her husband's entire estate to the Moravian Church."

"Are you saying that Mary Wendover Burnside is our Mystery Docent?" asked Adele with a twinkle in her eye.

"Stranger things have happened in Bethlehem, " said Mitzi. "I just wish that she would have been around to have given us a hand at the birth of little Jonathan!"

They continued to speculate about Mary Burnside and her interest in Bethlehem as they finished their lunch together.

"Do you think she'll make an appearance at Mark and Beth's open house this evening?" joked Sally. "Chris and I helped out with some of the beginning renovations. We had a great time, and... we even learned how to scrape off wallpaper! You're both going to be there, aren't you?"

"Zeke and I will be there," said Adele. "What about you and Vaughn?"

"We wouldn't miss it," said Mitzi, slipping on her coat. "I'm anxious to see what they've done so far. Elaine is thrilled that they bought the house from her. She's counting on a flock of future grandchildren living nearby."

If Mary Wendover Burnside happened not to attend the open house this evening, she would be the only one in Bethlehem who didn't, thought Adele. It was tough finding any parking spots left on the street when they arrived.

Mark greeted her and Zeke at the door. "Glad you could make it," he said. "Come on in."

Zeke shook Mark's hand and presented him with a bottle of wine. "I hope that this party doesn't get Adele thinking about renovating our house."

"Too late," smiled Adele. "Beth has given me some great decorating ideas."

Candles glowed at each of the windows; people gathered by the fireplace and clustered in the large kitchen. Strips of paint chips in warm colors and books of fabric swatches for new furniture were on display, ready for the guests to help make the final choices.

When Mitzi and Vaughn arrived just a few moments later, Mitzi and Adele both wanted to see the attic, since Beth had talked so much about it. The attic was one area that they managed to finish in the short time since they bought the house.

"You come too, Sally," said Beth, taking her hand and leading them up the two flights of stairs to the attic.

"This is so beautiful!" said Mitzi. "A master bedroom and a sitting room all in one!"

"We were fortunate to be able to make use of this space," said Beth. "And when Mark and I first started poking around to see what could be done, we made a neat discovery." She reached down to the coffee table in the sitting area and picked up a brightly painted figurine.

"How do you like our Wise Man?" she asked. "He was wrapped in newspaper and actually slid down inside the wall while we were sitting here one afternoon."

"He's wonderful," said Mitzi, taking the figurine from Beth. Weighing it in her hand she said, "Good heavens, he's heavy, too. Must be made of cast iron."

"I wish that we would have found more treasures in the walls," Beth said. "Mark and I would love to set up our own putz. We even have the room for it downstairs. We actually started constructing the platform, but we're running out of time to try to finish it this year. Plus, we need more putz figures, obviously."

"I'm sure that you'll find plenty of help in that department," said Adele. Looking around the new attic sitting room she said admiringly, "You've just done an amazing amount of work already. I like that you've included some interesting decorative touches. Very cozy! The apron and haube on the rocker in the corner are just perfect."

"Apron and haube?" said Beth. "Where? Oh. Maybe Mark put them out while I was in the kitchen. I don't remember seeing them before. That was a nice touch. He's so thoughtful," she said, smiling. "Well, let's get back to the party, shall we?"

The women began to make their way back downstairs as Mitzi quietly walked over to the rocker, reached down and turned over the hem of the soft, white apron.

SOME mysteries should not be explained away. Some Mystery Docents just seem to evaporate in the light of day. Or perhaps they are just overshadowed, at least for a time, by greater mysteries.

The Christmas season in Bethlehem that year reached a crescendo with the two magnificent Christmas Eve Vigil services in Central Moravian Church. From the gentle notes of "Stille Nacht," played by a guitarist, to the stirring anthems and the singing of "Morning Star, O Cheering Sight," by the congregation and a child soloist, the services brought their special gifts of peace, joy, love and hope to all who attended.

Lighted beeswax candles trimmed in red paper cast a soft glow across the sanctuary as Adele and Sally led the congregation in the final hymn and benediction.

Each Christmas in this city, thought Adele, is so familiar, yet so new at the same time. The story of the Christ Child continues to be told through scripture and music and all of the wonderful trappings of the season, but also through compassion to those in need and through the love of family and friends, from one generation to the next.

Old Bethlehem Christmas Mysteries

Book Two

Who Stole the Wise Men?

Putz - An arrangement of miniature figures in various Biblical scenes telling the story of the birth of Jesus.

The Phone Call

THE phone was ringing in her dream. "The phone is ringing and it's for you," Vaughn whispered in her ear. She sat bolt upright in bed. "OH NO! The phone is ringing." It was 3 am and that meant only one thing: something was wrong at one of her sites! Vaughn knew not to answer the phone when it rang during the night. It was always for Mitzi.

"Yes, This is Mitzi. Yes, I will be outside."

She turned to Vaughn, "Some one tried to break into the Moravian Museum. The police are coming to pick me up so that I can turn off the alarm and check the building."

Over all these years, there had never been a problem, but she knew the drill. There was always a first time and she hoped this was not it. Everything was almost ready for the Christmas season and Mitzi didn't want any problems.

"Good evening, Officer, or is it morning?" she said as she got into the back of the police car. It was always unnerving to see that there were no door handles.

The nice young officer drove her to the Moravian Museum where he and the other officer asked her to turn off the alarm and then stay back while they walked through the Museum, room by room. She followed them to the entrance door to each floor.

There were five levels in this Landmark building. She was so nervous. They had their guns ready for any intruders. Occasionally she would hear their handcuffs jangle quietly as they moved stealthily around the exhibits. She almost felt as if she were still dreaming, except this was real and they were deadly serious walking through the shadowy structure, the oldest building in the city made of hand-hewn, white oak logs, with its creaks and moans. These sounds seemed more ominous now, not just the typical sounds coming from an old building on a windy November night.

"No sign of any one."

"Thank goodness!"

Once the officers finished with their walk-through, being certain that no one was lurking in the shadows, Mitzi walked around with them again to ensure that nothing was missing or out of place. She really appreciated their sensitivity to her historic buildings. All the exterior doors and windows were intact and nothing had been disturbed.

"Another false alarm," she said to the officers. "Someone must have jiggled one of the handles of these 275 year old doors and set off the alarm."

"With so many visitors starting to come into town, this is to be expected," her young officer commiserated, and with that she got back in the police car for the drive home. Curiously, her neighbors never mentioned seeing her picked up or dropped off by the police in the middle of the night. Mitzi assumed they were being polite.

CHAPTER TWO

A Package Arrives

THE blustery fall wind was blowing the last of the leaves off the trees along Church Street as Baxter walked hurriedly to the Church office. With this brutal wind, you can tell that winter is on its way, he thought to himself.

"Good morning, Baxter. We weren't expecting to see you today."

"Hi Margaret. I'm just delivering a package that was mistakenly dropped off at the Widows' House. Delivery people do get confused by all of our buildings along this street, since so many of them are made of limestone and have that same colonial Germanic architectural style. From what I can see, the name and address seem to be "C.M. Church at 61 West Church Street," but there is no return address, just a lot of German stamps. The handwriting is not very clear. No one by that name lives at the Widows' House, so the ladies thought it must belong to Central Moravian Church."

"What's in the package?" chimed in Adele, hearing the commotion and coming out from her office.

"We'll find out," said Margaret as she sliced deftly through all the tape and threw away the sticky wrapping. There were several pieces inside. "Someone really didn't want anything to happen to whatever these are."

They each took one of the smaller packages that they found inside, carefully wrapped in multiple layers of paper and found that there were three beautifully painted Wise Men made of some sort of metal. At the bottom of the box, they found three more packages that turned out to contain three charming camels.

"Does anyone see any note in all of this paper?"

Margaret quickly rummaged through all the tissue paper wrapping that had been put in the recycling bin. "Nothing here!"

"I'm sure that we'll get an email from one of our fellow congregations in Germany telling us that they sent us these lovely figurines for our community putz. Someone will be expecting us to acknowledge the gift," commented Adele. "It was so generous of them to send it."

Baxter started examining the figures more carefully. "I wonder when were they made. They're rather heavy; they must be made of lead." Setting down the figures he said, "Well, I'm sure that the ladies in the Widows' House will be coming over to see what was in the mystery package."

"Margaret, we'll give the pieces to our volunteers to add to the putz, but let's just put them up here on the fireplace mantel for now, since we might have curious neighbors stopping in this afternoon," Adele said with a wry smile.

Baxter pulled up his collar as he was about to venture out the door. "See you later, ladies. That wind is so strong today. I'll try not to let any leaves blow in the door!"

CHAPTER THREE

Prepping for the Christmas Season

O N a cold, dark November afternoon, Mitzi was looking out her office window watching the snow flurries and the gently flowing Monocacy Creek. This bodes well for the Christmas season, she thought; the snow is adding that bit of childhood wonder and painting a beautiful picture for all the tourists who will be coming into Bethlehem in the coming weeks. *Some* snow is great, but lots of snow will shut down the city and drive away the needed tourist revenue.

Bethlehem, Pennsylvania she pondered... it really was a special place. Christened on Christmas Eve 1741 in a stable. Almost sounds like a movie.

Well, there was work to do, she had to tell herself, not just gazing out the window. This was the busiest time of year for her and her staff and volunteers. They all worked hard but also had fun decorating all the museums and historic sites. New as well as returning guides were trying on their winter costumes, making sure that they had all the pieces: haubes, aprons, hats, vests, capes and cloaks against the winter cold - transforming themselves into inhabitants of early Moravian Bethlehem.

Volunteers chose different themes each year for all the Christmas trees and Laura, her curator, coordinated the holiday exhibits. Electrified candles with white lights were placed in every window. Moravian stars were hung from porches. Christmas was coming once again and now it was time to make sure all the visitors, residents and tourists alike, had a fabulous time during the holidays. As night fell, the star on South Mountain would be shining down upon the city.

Just then, Fred Lang and Rodrigo Carnarvon came bounding into her office, bringing her back to reality. She had to admit that she was still tired after her middle of the night escapade with the false alarm.

"Mitzi, can you believe it's that time of year again? We're here to pick up the putz figures. Rodrigo and I have everything ready; the moss and driftwood are in place; just have to add the figures."

Many people decorated their homes with Nativity scenes, but Moravians in particular created elaborate scenes called putzes, telling the entire biblical Christmas story in miniature.

Rodrigo, a bank executive, was an incredible putz designer and sometimes included "unauthorized" scenes, or added pieces just for fun, to trick the visitors. Fred was Fred, a retired engineer and dedicated researcher for the Society; they were two of her favorite volunteers. Volunteers, of course, were the lifeblood of their institutions.

"I asked Laura to bring the putz figures out of the vault so that you two can arrange the scenes at the Moravian Museum and the Single Sisters' House. I can't wait to see what you come up with this year! It always makes me feel like Christmas when we put up the putzes and the Christmas trees."

Fred, who sometimes helped as a docent during the holidays, said, "You know, Mitzi, we guides love to wear costumes and we always enjoy explaining the story behind the Moravian putz. And having the visitors guess what's out of the ordinary!"

"You two always create such fantastic putzes for us with so many different biblical scenes."

"We have great material to work with, don't we?" commented Rodrigo. "The Museum's figures are fabulous. I feel like we're touching history when we use pieces that were so lovingly collected by families and then handed down from generation to generation. The Moravian Museum is very fortunate to have so many sets of putz figures. Fred and I have a great time mixing it up!"

There were many, many putz figures in the Museum's inventory, so Rodrigo always made sure that the sizes were correct and in proportion to each other. "We can't have one Wise Man twice as big as the other Wise Men, or sheep bigger that the camels. All these figures are from different sets and are all different sizes."

Some of the donated figures were beautifully hand carved wood, some of lead, some of plaster, and some made of wax. Mitzi's husband Vaughn had even donated his mother's antique, miniature wooly sheep to the Museum's collection of putz figures.

The fact that not everything matched made it that much more interesting as Rodrigo and Fred put together the scenes at various places around the Society's historic buildings. They draped long tables with dark fabric and created mountains out of hand-painted rock paper. They re-used the old logs and driftwood and stones from many generations of putz makers. But the one thing that was new every year was the moss.

Each year local Moravian families participated in the annual field trip on a Sunday afternoon in November, to the mountains north of town to gather fresh, green, lush moss. This was one of the Christmas traditions that continued again and again. Fred and Rodrigo and their families also took part in the outing, collecting moss for the putzes at the Moravian Churches and for the museums.

CHAPTER FOUR

Thanksgiving, Already?

THANKSGIVING is upon us, Adele was thinking, hoping that Zeke picked up the flowers for their dining room table, as she bumped into Mitzi on Church Street. "Are you ready?"

"Are *you* ready?" They both laughed. This was the busiest time for the Church as well. Adele was the Senior Pastor of Central Moravian Church and Mitzi was the President of the Bethlehem Historical Society.

"I think everything is ready," commented Mitzi. "The stage is set; the Christmas season is about to begin. Our volunteers have decorated all the museums exquisitely once again this year. Rodrigo and Fred have all the putz figures in place." Fred and Rodrigo also helped with the very large community putz in the Church's Christian Education building. Buses came from far and wide to visit Bethlehem and to see the Moravian Church putzes as well as all the museums.

"I forgot to tell you about the package that Baxter brought to the Church office last week." Adele recounted the story of unpacking the Wise Men and camels. "We still don't know who sent them, but they came from Germany. I gave them to the guys, for them to use in one of the scenes of the Church's putz."

"Oh, I'll have to run up to the CE Building and see them when I get a chance," responded Mitzi with excitement.

"Let's meet to review the bus schedule again, shall we? I know that there will be changes right after Thanksgiving."

Out of town tour groups often had to make last minute changes to their schedules depending upon weather, restaurant reservations, or whatever. The Church and Society had been working together for years helping visitors plan their various activities and services during the holiday season.

Mitzi was very fortunate that Brett and Cecelia, Vaughn's parents, loved coming down to Bethlehem from Connecticut. They helped get Thanksgiving dinner and gave her a day off before the rush.

Black Friday dawned cold but beautiful, the perfect weather to be out. Mitzi checked in with her staff at the Kemerer Museum, Moravian Museum, Single Sisters' House, Goundie House, Burnside Plantation, and Blacksmith Shop. All the museums were ready to open their doors at 10 am; the docents were in place in their historic costumes, ready to share stories of years gone by. The Christmas season began once again as visitors from all over the world descended on Bethlehem of Pennsylvania.

Late that afternoon was the lighting of the community Christmas Tree. At 6 pm, the lights on all the city trees would go on, with lighted Christmas trees at all of the intersections around the city. Mitzi and Adele decided to check in briefly after the lighting.

All the residents got into the spirit of the season, putting lighted electrified candles in their windows and decorating their homes. Bethlehem was dressed in its finest and ready for Christmas.

CHAPTER FIVE

Back in Town

Now that she had moved back to Bethlehem, Beth Ettwein decided once again to be a docent for Mitzi and to help Adele at the Church wherever she could. Bethlehem at Christmas was so special; she missed it very much while she was living in Chicago. Now she was sharing it with her fiancé Mark, too.

She was delighted that Mitzi asked her to be the docent at the Single Sisters' House, since her family traced its roots to early Bethlehem and some of her ancestors actually lived in the building at one time. She loved being in this place; she felt so at home here. She always tried to imagine what it must have been like to live here over the centuries. What if the walls could really talk!

"Good afternoon and welcome to the Single Sisters' House," she said to a group of visitors entering the large wooden door with its heavy iron strap hinges. She enjoyed greeting the guests and seeing old friends who came back each year with their families for the beloved Christmas traditions.

Rodrigo and Fred had outdone themselves, having set the putzes on tables winding their way in and out of rooms. They kept the lights low, with quiet Christmas music playing in the background, giving a serene, calming atmosphere. Visitors instinctively lowered their voices as they walked along the same clay tile floors that women had walked for almost 275 years. They oohed and aahhed and giggled occasionally, on seeing a miniature lamppost here or an ice skater there in the middle of the Arabian desert scene.

The visitors left and Beth was alone again with the quiet music and the wind rattling the old windows. Something was odd this afternoon, though. She thought that she kept seeing a shadow at the end of the long hall, but wondered why would there be a shadow there. Her mind was just playing tricks on her. It was a dark, windy late afternoon and it was probably the wind creating patterns from the shadows of trees, or people walking by outside, she thought to herself.

Just then the door opened and a young couple entered with their tickets. "Welcome," Beth said, as she looked into the man's piercing blue eyes, at first striking, and then surprisingly rather cold. The woman beside him was absolutely beautiful and fabulously dressed, she thought to herself as she checked their tickets. She saw that they had purchased passes that would allow them to return during the season.

"We are fascinated with your putz traditions," commented the woman rather solemnly. "Please follow me," Beth said "we have a good number of scenes from the biblical Christmas story to show you."

"Are all your figures from the same collection or the same maker?" The man's voice had a deep timbre - was it friendly or not? Beth wasn't sure as she thought before she answered. She could not imagine why she had such a strange feeling in the pit of her stomach. Was she just looking at a beautiful couple or was there something unsettling about them?

"Oh no," she said hoping that she hadn't hesitated too long. "These were collected by many families and were made at various times, in different countries, and using different materials. We are very fortunate here at the Moravian Museum that so many families decided to donate some or all of their treasured pieces to us for everyone to enjoy at Christmas time."

After the couple left, while there was a lull in visitation, she called Mitzi. "There was a well-dressed young couple lingering around the putzes this afternoon. They seemed nice enough, so I feel a little guilty about this, but I'm a bit suspicious of them."

"This is all very odd" commented Mitzi. "Billy just mentioned that the same thing happened at the Moravian Museum as he was giving one of his tours today.

"Since we have our holiday season passes that give visitors the opportunity to come back to their favorite places, you may see them again. Perhaps they are just enjoying Christmas in Bethlehem. Let's just continue to observe."

I wonder who they are, and why they are so interested in the putz figures, Mitzi thought.

On her rounds from site to site, Mitzi stopped at the Society's Visitor Center and Museum Store on Main Street to check in with Kim, their site manager there. "All the shop people on the street are commenting about a lovely young couple who are so exquisitely dressed stopping in the shops." Kim said excitedly. "I saw them from a distance. They look like New York City models walking along. I heard that he has gorgeous, piercing blue eyes and she looks like she is the kind of woman you see on the pages of a high-end fashion magazine. Every article of clothing seemed to have a logo on it. When they walk by, people stop and stare at them. I hope they come into our Visitor Center!"

CHAPTER SIX

A Putz Watcher

HER secretary Margaret buzzed, "Adele, we just got a call from the putz watcher at the Christian Education Building about our Church putz. Evidently a young couple came in on Friday and then again today to look at it. They asked some unusual questions about the figures. Just wanted to let you know that it seemed rather odd."

"Families do go "putzing" every year to visit all the different putzes. When I was a young girl, we used to go putzing at each other's homes and churches. Families certainly come back, as a tradition year after year, but they generally only come once each year. Yes, this is definitely rather strange." Adele said.

"I think I may have seen that couple when I went out to lunch yesterday," replied Margaret, "they were very striking looking."

Very curious, Adele thought as she returned to her office. Who is this couple?

It was rather unusual for visitors who came for the Thanksgiving weekend to still be in town the following week. She decided to ask Mitzi if she knew anything about the couple when she came in later to review the tour schedule.

But for now, she had to get ready for the Advent Lovefeast, which this year fell a week later. Regardless of the timing, Advent Sunday was truly the start of the season for her and the Church.

Roger, who was the Tour Manager and worked at her Visitor Center helping with all the Christmas activities, called Mitzi excitedly. "We finally know the names of that young couple. Their names are Clayton and Valerie and they have signed up for the 7 pm Night Light bus tour this evening."

"Roger, did you get their address as well?"

"No, they paid in cash for the bus tour and gave a New York City zip code. But I was watching them as they strolled around the store. I did hear their first names because while they were looking around the museum store, they called out to each other commenting on various items. Then, would you believe it, they bought one of our 3 scene *plastic* putzes. Can you imagine plastic putzes! But again they paid with cash. They don't seem to be the plastic putz type, from the way they're dressed and from the money that Clayton had in his wallet. Why would anyone be carrying around so much cash?"

"Thanks for being so observant, Roger. It's helpful to know more about them."

Curiouser and curiouser, Mitzi thought, and then immediately called Adele. "Remember our discussing the drop dead gorgeous couple who have been strolling along Main Street? Well, Billy, our docent at the Moravian Museum mentioned again that this couple keeps coming back to look at the putzes. They seemed interested at first, but now Billy said it seemed downright suspicious to him that they are always hanging around in the putz room in the Gemeinhaus."

"Mitzi, we got the same comments from our putz watcher in the Christian Education Building."

"Well, how would you like to go on the bus tour this evening and do a little detective work?"

Roger reserved two seats for them on the same 7 pm bus tour.

CHAPTER SEVEN

The Bus Ride

AT 7 pm that evening, Mitzi and Adele found themselves standing in line for the Night Light bus tour. They pretended to be tourists and maneuvered their way to sit behind the couple.

Mitzi had already notified the guide not to pay any attention to her and Adele, to just treat them as any other tourists. The guides were used to seeing Mitzi on the bus tours, walking tours, or in the museums. She was all over during the Christmas season, checking that everything was working and that visitors were enjoying their experiences. It was extremely important to fix any issues immediately.

"Don't tell Zeke that we are sleuthing again," Adele whispered to Mitzi. "He warned me to stay out of trouble, but I told him that trouble always finds us!"

Unfortunately, try as they might, Mitzi and Adele could not hear any conversation from the couple, who were silent as the bus took them all around the town. The tour guide in period Moravian dress explained all the local Christmas customs as the bus wound its way through the streets of Bethlehem.

"No matter how often I take this tour,"said Adele, "it is always so enjoyable to see all the lights - the white lights on the north side of town and then the beautiful multi-colored lights on the south side of the Lehigh River."

When the tour ended, Clayton and Valerie turned and smiled at Mitzi and Adele as they stood up to exit the bus. Then the couple disappeared in the crowd of evening shoppers and diners on the street.

"Well, that was fun, but we know nothing more that we did before. What was that glint of metal at the top of his coat pocket? Did you see that?"

"Adele you're imagining things. It wasn't a gun, if that's what you're thinking - it was probably a very expensive pocket watch!"

"Maybe I'm still a little 'gun-shy' since our run-in with that Norman Sterner at the Tannery last year!" Adele and Mitzi could finally laugh about that scary situation, but hoped that something like that was a once in a lifetime event.

CHAPTER EIGHT

Tickets Are Needed

T HE next morning, Adele walked into the Church office and had to control her surprise on seeing Clayton and Valerie speaking with her secretary, Margaret. She hoped that they didn't recognize her as she ducked quietly into her office.

"Our Advent Lovefeast takes place this Sunday. It is a very popular service of prayers and singing to begin the Advent season in our Moravian Church. Everyone also receives a sugar bun and cup of coffee during the service. It is really a high-point and start of the season," she overheard Margaret explaining to the couple.

Then one of them mumbled something.

"Yes, you do need tickets, but they're free. Would you like to join us on Sunday? Here are two tickets. Would you be interested in receiving information about our Church or other events here?"

Very good Margaret, Adele said to herself.

She didn't hear a response. Then the door opened and closed and then opened again a minute later.

Baxter's booming voice echoed in the hallway, "Margaret, what a lovely couple. They told me they are coming on Sunday. Did you get their contact information? Do they live in the area? I wonder if they would like to come to an Inquirer's Class."

Adele came out of her office to greet him. Pastor Baxter Hemphill, who was semi-retired, was always trying to share the history of the Church and gently encourage people to become members. He and his wife Ramona were such an engaging couple in the community.

As Baxter and Adele started back to her office to review the Christmas schedule, Margaret commented, "I tried to start a conversation with them, but no luck! They just said that they really liked Bethlehem."

After she and Baxter finished their meeting, Adele decided to give Mitzi a call. "Mitzi, this is so very curious, but maybe everyone is being too suspicious of Clayton and Valerie. Maybe these gorgeous young people are simply taken with Bethlehem at Christmas. They are coming to the Advent Lovefeast on Sunday."

"Adele, let's consider a few things: where are they staying? don't they have jobs? They've been seen at various times and locations around town since Thanksgiving and not just on the weekend."

"Are you sure you aren't being overly concerned? They may have taken an extended vacation or perhaps they really are high-end models and have some time off between photo shoots!"

"We aren't savvy enough about that world, my dear!" Adele never liked it when Mitzi called them "two women of a certain age."

Adele decided to phone her favorite young couple, Beth Ettwein and Mark Sargent, to find out if they knew anything about the two new people in town. Had they seen them anywhere or heard anything about them?

"I have seen them several times at the Single Sisters' House to look at the putzes," Beth explained. "But Mark hasn't had the pleasure. I've never experienced visitors coming back so many times!"

"Well, when you come to Advent Lovefeast, maybe you can chat with them before or after the service."

"Are you and Mitzi being detectives again?" laughed Mark in the background. "I can't wait to see this couple!"

CHAPTER NINE

The Advent Lovefeast

ADVENT Lovefeast was the perfect start to the religious season of Christmas. It was one of Adele's favorites - a service of singing and sharing of refreshments together: a sugar bun and cup of coffee.

Adele walked into the Sanctuary along with their young Pastor Sally, and Baxter, who always assisted during the holidays. Adele took her seat behind the pulpit and just as the service was about to begin, she saw the mysterious Clayton and Valerie ushered to seats, by chance, along with Mark and Beth. Adele hoped that her surprise couldn't be seen by the congregation, although she was adept at hiding her personal feelings. A pastor had to be that way.

When the service ended, Mark and Beth walked out with the couple, chatting as they left the Church.

"Well, who are they?" Adele and Mitzi cornered Beth and Mark outside after the service.

Mark said, "They told us they are taking some time off work to explore and get to know the town, and may consider moving here from New York City. They didn't mention what they did, but they obviously have lots of money from they way they were talking. And she dropped a $100 bill in the offering plate! They seemed very pleasant to me. I told them that we loved living in Bethlehem and that we bought a house last year and are fixing it up. They asked about real estate prices here in town. I wondered if they really are thinking of moving here from NYC?"

"I don't know about that. You are too trusting, Mark, telling them all about us. They seemed a bit fake, not genuine to me," commented Beth. "They never even realized that I was the one who showed them the putz several times."

"You were in costume. I don't even recognize you when you're dressed as a Moravian Sister!"

Laughing, Beth and Mark said their goodbyes and left to continue decorating their new home for the holidays.

Beth and Mark had bought an historic home a few blocks away, just before the holiday season last year and had been spending their spare time restoring it. Mitzi and Adele were so pleased that Beth and Mark found each other - such a loving couple, but Adele was eager to perform the wedding ceremony. They were engaged, but no date set as yet.

CHAPTER TEN

The Buses Arrive

THE first two weeks of December were the busiest with bus tour groups from out of the area. There were so many groups coming today that Mitzi herself was helping with the tours, checking the sites, opening and closing the buildings before and after the tours, greeting visitors, doing whatever needed to be done.

Her next stop was the Single Sisters' House to turn off the alarm, and turn on the lights and quiet music for a group about to arrive.

Every time she walked into this building she was struck by the sense of peace and felt surrounded by warmth. Women had lived here for hundreds of years.

All of a sudden she thought she saw a shadow down the hall. Beth did mention a shadow at the end of the hall, didn't she? The building was not haunted, at least not by bad spirits, she thought to herself. In a minute, there will be a bus full of tourists here. I'll definitely investigate later.

Glancing at one of the putz scenes, she noticed that one of the Wise Men was missing. That's odd, she thought. She sent a text to Laura noting that the piece was missing. I wonder if it fell on the floor under the draping, she thought to herself. She didn't have time to look for it, or find another.

Just then, the door opened and 50 eager tourists from across the state came in, anticipating their Bethlehem Christmas experience. As each few moved into the space, they quieted themselves, sensing something special in this atmosphere. The group didn't seem to notice a missing Wise Man. They appreciated the setting, the quiet music, and the simplicity.

After helping her staff with several tours at different sites, Mitzi stopped in the Church office to check schedules for the coming few days.

A number of groups had changes. Sometimes it was just easier to meet in person than to mark up the spreadsheet and send it out.

The Church office was a very cozy, welcoming space with a fireplace mantle decorated with a hand-carved wooden nativity set from Jerusalem, candles in the windows and in the distance, the music of the church organist practicing for the service on Sunday.

"Margaret, is Adele available? I have a few more changes in the tour schedule." Mitzi was always careful not to interrupt, in case Adele was in a counseling session.

"She is working on her message for Sunday. I will let her know you're here."

Margaret knocked on the door to Adele's office, "Sorry to interrupt, but Mitzi is here."

"Oh, it's never an interruption when Mitzi comes to our office! Please have her come in right away."

Mitzi stepped into Adele's office and closed the door before she spoke. "Adele, I have another mystery, after we check the schedule. Would you believe that one of our Wise Men is missing from one of the putz scenes in the Single Sisters' House? I was so busy this afternoon, I didn't have a chance to go back and look to see if it simply fell on the floor. You know with all that draping, it could have been kicked under one of the tables. But, have you had any missing putz figures or have you heard if there are any missing at any of the other churches?"

"No. This has never happened before. People have always been so respectful of these putz scenes. Perhaps it's simply on the floor, or someone picked it up to look at it and put the Wise Man in another scene."

"Our volunteers always watch carefully and our visitors never even try to pick up any of the figures."

"After we make the tour changes, I'll come help you look."

All the tourists had gone to dinner and candles were shining in all the windows giving a warm glow to the street. The museums were closed for the night, but the staff was busy with visitors now taking the candlelight walking tours or the bus tours to experience the ambience of Bethlehem at night.

A gentle snow was falling as Adele and Mitzi crossed the quiet street to the Single Sisters' House. A group of visitors bundled against the snow was listening intently as one of Mitzi's docents, portraying an early Moravian and carrying a lighted, wooden lantern, shared stories of Christmas past in Bethlehem. The groan of the heavy door interrupted the peaceful scene.

"Remind me to have those old iron hinges oiled. Hold on - did you just see that shadow at the end of the hall?"

The only light came from the single candles in each window casting shadows on the walls as the wind rattled the old windows.

"Now, Mitzi, there aren't any ghosts here. And they aren't stealing any figures. No, I didn't see any weird shadow."

Mitzi and Adele made there way down the hall to the rooms with the putzes. The sound of their footsteps echoed as they walked on the old clay tile floor. Under their feet, they could feel how the tiles were worn down by all the years of the women walking these very halls.

"Fred and Rodrigo do such a fabulous job creating all these scenes," Adele commented as she peeked into each of the rooms. "I wonder what the ladies who once lived here would think of their living spaces being used to show putz figures, and all of these visitors invading their homes this time of year."

In the early days, these were work rooms where the sisters did spinning and weaving. Later they became small apartments with one or two rooms and common restroom facilities - very much like a dormitory setting.

"Can't you feel a sense of warmth, even though it is rather cold and drafty in here?"

"It must have been very cold before modern heating systems."

When they entered the room with the missing Wise Man, Mitzi got down on her hands and knees, crawling under the tables with a flashlight hoping to find the missing piece.

"I'll look at all the scenes and see if there is anything out of place. I am sure it's here somewhere."

"Nothing here, just stray pieces of straw under the tables and the watering cans for the moss," she called out as she crawled along.

All of a sudden the exhibit lights went out. "Adele, are you there? What happened?"

No one answered her. "Adele, where are you?" Mitzi hit her head on the bottom of the table as she quickly tried to get out from under all the draping. She definitely didn't want to knock over all the work that Fred and Rodrigo had done to set up the putz scenes.

There were so many shadows from the candle light at the windows. The wind was picking up and the snow was heavier.

"Adele?"

"Mitzi, I saw a shadow at the end of the hall and I tried to see where it was coming from. Then the lights went out."

"The old dining room is at the end of the hall and there are no other doors. It is a dead end. Let me get the lights back on. I always hate when there is an electrical problem in this building. The breakers are in a closet in the basement and I hate going down there."

"Mitzi, there is nothing down there to be afraid of."

"I know, but that's where, according to the tales told to me, they stored the dead bodies of the ladies who had died in the winter when the ground was too frozen to dig and before they built the dead house."

Mitzi shone the light on the wooden stairs to the basement.

"It's rather creepy and there is a strange smell. Even though it is night outside, it is so dreadfully dark in here. With no windows it seems like a crypt. I can understand the storing of bodies - it is freezing down here."

"Haven't you ever been in here before, Adele?"

"Just for visits to the ladies, before it was turned into a museum. But never down here. This will be my first and last time going down these stairs. Why don't you get that electrical panel moved to the first floor?"

It was a very long, steep stairwell that creaked as they gingerly went down one step at a time; a rough stone wall on the one side and complete blackness on the other, with just a thin wooden railing to keep them from falling off into nothingness. It was almost as if the light from Mitzi's flashlight was swallowed up by the darkness. When they finally got to the bottom, they both jumped as a mouse scurried by their feet.

"I hope that was what I think it was! OK. Mitzi, where is that electrical panel so we can get the heck out of here!"

"Such language is so out of character for you, Pastor Adele! You must be as unnerved as I am about being down here."

As Mitzi shone her light around, the metal cover of the electrical panel reflected back at them with more shadows. Then Mitzi cried out, "What is going on here?"

She saw a heap of material - was it clothing on the damp dirt floor? Some articles of clothing dumped here by a former resident?

They looked around the room. No one was there and there was no place to hide. This was so strange.

"And what is that smell?"

"Was that the shadow that Beth saw and I saw earlier today?"

"Is someone hiding down here?"

"Let's get the lights on and get back upstairs. I will call our maintenance guys to clean this up and have this basement door locked and the panel moved."

"Did someone flip this breaker on purpose?" said Mitzi as the lights went on immediately.

Even with the lights on, the basement room was still rather scary with its dark, cold stone walls, hard-packed dirt floor and only a grated air vent near ground level. Their task accomplished, Mitzi and Adele dashed back upstairs and closed the door.

After catching their breath, Adele said to Mitzi, "Well, let me look again at the scenes, I got distracted."

"I'll keep looking under the tables."

After walking around, looking at the scenes more carefully, Adele called out, "Isn't a camel supposed to be here with the Wise Men?"

"Oh, no! Another piece missing! What is going on?" Mitzi called back. Suddenly she got very quiet. "Adele, I just saw that shadow at the end of the hall! Did you see it?" They walked quickly down the hall to the dining room. No one was there. Lots of windows, but no doors. They did not hear any sounds except the wind-blown snow brushing against the building.

"Someone is playing tricks on us, Mitzi! Maybe someone was outside making shadows through the windows to scare us. But then again, you know all these old buildings are interconnected if you know where to look."

"I had heard that too. But I never figured out exactly how to get around." After glancing out the window, "Adele, we'd better get out of here, the snow is really starting to pile up and we will have lots of calls tomorrow with delayed tours."

"Mitzi, are you okay to lock up? I will be right across the street in my office if you need me. I want to check with our maintenance crew about snow removal in the morning."

When Adele left, Mitzi walked slowly down the hall and sensed a strange, but not unpleasant smell, as if one of the residents were once again in her apartment cooking dinner. It actually made her hungry. I must be going crazy - shadows, lights going off, old clothes in the basement. She turned out the lights, set the alarm and walked out into the snowy night, not aware of the shadow still hovering behind her on the hallway wall.

Across town, early in the morning, a putz volunteer pulled back the curtain for the East Hills Moravian Church Putz to check the moss. It had to be watered frequently to keep it fresh and green. Looking over the scenes, the volunteer noticed an empty space where a figure should be. He scratched his head, looked on the floor and then behind the curtain. One of the Wise Men was nowhere to be found. Kids, he decided. A middle school group was here yesterday and, of course they were supervised, but there was always the opportunity to pull off some mischief, especially with these small figures.

CHAPTER ELEVEN

A Tall Tale

AFTER their adventure in the basement, Mitzi and Adele decided to re-group after they heard from the tour bus guides. The sun was shining and melting the snow already; it was going to be another busy but beautiful, crisp day.

"Mitzi, has Nellie Titherington told you the Golden Putz story?"

"I had heard the rumor of a Golden Putz, but I didn't know where that came from."

"Can you spare an hour to visit Nellie? I'll meet you there right after lunch. I'll bring along some sugar cake for her. She has a sweet tooth."

For years there had been rumors that somewhere among the Moravian family putzes, there was a putz made of gold. Nellie Titherington, one of the descendants from an old Moravian family, was told the story as a young girl. She was now 98 years old and holding court, telling her stories at Moravian Village retirement community to anyone who would listen.

Evidently during one of the many wars in Europe, one of the early Moravian families was trying to hold on to their resources, since the revolutionaries were ransacking every home looking for gold, silver and jewels.

The family had a toy-making business and had molds for many different types of lead soldiers and little dolls for the children of wealthy families to play with.

The father melted down their meager savings of gold coins and made a Moravian putz and then painstakingly painted all the golden figures, hoping that the soldiers would not bother a simple toy maker until he had finished his desperate project. He wanted to get his family out of harm's way and the putz figures could be their escape.

As Nellie was telling her story, everyone was hanging on every word. "So what happened, Nellie?"

"Are you sure this really happened?" a skeptical person asked.

Nellie just shook her head. "No one has ever found the Golden Putz, but I am sure that it exists."

Another resident asked, " What was the family name? What ever happened to the family?"

"No one knows the answer to that." But Nellie was certain that the story was true.

Adele and Mitzi were standing nearby listening to the story once again. "Do you really think that someone believes that the Golden Putz is here in Bethlehem?" asked Mitzi.

After she was finished, Adele and Mitzi enjoyed sugar cake with Nellie as they told her about the missing Wise Man and camel.

Early that evening at Moravian Village, residents were lining up to go into dinner. Nellie Titherington stopped to look at the putz in the lobby. The scenes were made with figures that she and her late husband had brought back from Oberammergau in Germany, many years ago. Looking at them reminded her of all the good times they had together, over so many years of marriage. She was glad to share her putz figures with the rest of the residents. The figures were so beautifully hand-carved, with wonderful expressions on the faces, and actually rather valuable. But Nellie didn't care about the money, she valued the sentiment as a reminder of the life that she and her husband had enjoyed.

Incredibly, something was wrong - one of the Wise Men was missing. She asked the nice, young desk attendant to check on the floor. She looked over the various scenes and no Wise Man. She couldn't imagine that any of the senior residents here would take one of the figures. Before going into dinner, she notified the management about the missing figure. "Perhaps it was swept up. We'll check with the cleaning service."

After dinner, Nellie called Adele with the news.

CHAPTER TWELVE

Missing Pieces

Adele was still in her office waiting for a counseling session with a young couple about to be married. I wonder when Beth and Mark will decide to marry, she thought to herself as she was preparing her notes, when the call came in from Nellie.

After her counseling session was over, she called Mitzi to pass along Nellie's report. "Mitzi, I think it's time for our Detective Team to go into action!"

The next day, Adele called around to the other churches and sure enough, something was missing from each putz: sometimes a Wise Man and sometimes a camel. She walked up to the Christian Education Building to meet with the putz volunteers. Baxter was there having coffee with the group before the start of another day of visitors.

"Nothing missing here," Baxter boomed. "And you all were so suspicious of that nice young couple!"

One of the fellows spoke between sips of coffee, "Haven't seen that nice couple around lately though. They *seemed* suspicious, but I guess they were just really curious."

"Thefts are very unusual for our community, even with all the visitors," one of the other volunteers commented. "Whoever is doing this must not like our putz." Everyone laughed and then sighed, sorry for the sad situation.

Later Mitzi, Vaughn, Adele and Zeke took a brief respite to have a glass of wine and supper in one of the restaurants on Main Street.

"Why a Wise Man and a camel? Do you think any one really believes Nellie's story about a Golden Putz and was stealing what they hoped were golden figures?"

"If it does exist, it could be anywhere in the world. Why here? And besides, the figures are so small, how much could one possibly be worth if it is made of gold?"

"Vaughn, you're a finance person. Can you figure out how much it might be worth?"

"There are too many questions to answer that. What was the quality of the gold? How many pieces did the toy-maker make?"

So far, nothing was missing from the Central Church putz and nothing from the Moravian Museum.

"Isn't that Mark and Beth going into that new restaurant that just opened up across the street?" asked Zeke.

From her seat by the window, Mitzi could see that it was Mark and Beth. "It is so nice that Mark and Beth are settling in here in Bethlehem." Just as she spoke, she saw the New York couple go into the same restaurant. She gave a furtive look across the table to Adele.

"Yes," said Vaughn, "Bethlehem is such a nice place for a young couple to live, make new friends, and begin a family."

"Do you two know something we don't know?" Zeke asked Vaughn.

"No, I was just making conversation, Zeke. But who knows? Young people of today!"

Vaughn and Zeke started chuckling.

"Now you two boys just stop that. I'm still waiting for Mark and Beth to set a date for the wedding," chastised Adele, laughing.

As they left the restaurant, Adele quietly asked Mitzi, "What did you see when you gave me that look? I couldn't see anything with my back to the window."

"Clayton and Valerie went into that restaurant right after Mark and Beth."

CHAPTER THIRTEEN

A Young Thief Confesses

ADELE was working on her message for Sunday when Margaret told her that one of her confirmation class students was calling and needed to speak with her right away.

"Pastor Adele, I need to speak with you where no one will see us." This is an odd request, she thought. Teenagers could sometimes be so dramatic, but she was concerned about this young man who lived in a difficult family situation. "Stevie, why don't you come to my office. It's safe here."

"Something bad is going on and I don't know what to do. I can't tell you; it's too dangerous, but someone is trying to get me to steal."

"Stevie, I am at the Church office. Come right now." It was 3:30 in the afternoon; he must be on his way home from school, she thought. Was he the one stealing putz figures? Maybe the missing putz figure case is solved. But how was she going to help this young man? He sounded extremely nervous about being seen.

About 15 minutes later he appeared at the office, clutching a paper bag. "Come in Stevie. There is nothing to be afraid of." They stepped to the back of the hallway to talk.

"Pastor Adele, I'm too scared to tell you, but this person is trying to get me to steal putz figures. I know that it's wrong, but he threatened to hurt my mother if I don't do it."

Adele realized that this was not a prank by Stevie and some of his friends, but a more serious situation. The police and social services would have to be involved.

"Why don't you just return all the pieces to me?"

"I only stole 3 camels and I got scared. I don't want to do this. Here are the camels. Please don't report me."

"Where are the Wise Men?"

"I didn't steal any Wise Men."

"Why were you supposed to steal the camels?"

"This person told me they were made of gold and he wanted to melt them down and sell the gold."

"Oh Stevie...that is just an old tale. Please tell me who this person is so that I can help you and your family."

"NO!"

"Then tell the person that I took the camels from you when you were in my confirmation class."

As soon as Stevie left, Adele pondered the best course of action to protect Stevie and his family. With the camels returned, she decided not to call the police, but she would notify social services to keep a watchful eye on the family.

Now, where were the Wise Men?

The next morning Adele called the other churches and Mitzi to let them know that the camels had been found, without revealing how. She would keep Stevie's secret, at least for now.

CHAPTER FOURTEEN

Some Research to Do

FOR the Historical Society, the only piece missing at the moment was the Wise Man from the Single Sisters' House putz. Nothing from the putz in the Moravian Museum.

Mitzi and Laura checked the Society's detailed putz donation records. All the pieces were from old Moravian families. Some of the families came to Bethlehem in the early days of the settlement in the 1740's. The pieces had been handed down in these families until the mid-1900's when people began donating their extensive, multi-scene putz figures to the Museum or to one of the local Moravian churches. But according to the files, they were all made of wood, lead, plaster, or wax.

Mitzi called Peter Johansen, archivist for the Moravian Church, to see if any of the early family names included in the Society's donor forms matched any records of the early families in the archives. None of the families seemed to have anything to do with toy-making.

Mitzi then contacted Fred and Rodrigo to meet her in the Moravian Museum to look at all the figures in the collection.

They picked up each one. Some were heavier than others, some larger, some smaller, but yes, wood, plaster, metal of some kind, and wax. They always thought they were made of hand-carved wood, or lead poured into molds.

"We don't want to scratch off the paint to see if any of these metal ones are gold?" asked Fred.

"I don't want to damage them in any way," warned Mitzi.

Meanwhile, Adele was contacting all the other churches to check their putz figures.

If Stevie only stole the camels, what happened to the Wise Men? Was someone else made to steal them? From their conversation, Stevie really didn't know. Adele was sure that he would have told her if one of his friends was being forced to steal.

What about by Clayton and Valerie? Or were they were too obvious to be suspects?

Nothing more happened for the next few weeks of the season. Mitzi and Adele thought the situation was solved. Maybe it really was Stevie and his friends and he would not admit that they stole the Wise Men, too. They probably scratched off the paint or broke the wooden ones and saw that they were lead or wood, nothing more.

The bus groups were winding down; it was now just before Christmas. Most people wanted to be near home and family. The streets of Bethlehem were filled with locals doing their Christmas shopping in the boutique stores, dining at the restaurants or just strolling the streets.

Meanwhile, Clayton and Valerie who were seen in town around Thanksgiving with such a flurry of interest seemed to have disappeared. And then, just as suddenly, a few days before Christmas they were back again, walking on Main Street or visiting the putzes.

Roger, who was dating one of the staff at Hotel Bethlehem, told Mitzi that they had reserved rooms at the Hotel for the Christmas season. No one was sure why they were back, or why were they coming or going or where they went. It was a topic of much interest among the staff of the Hotel.

Beth and Mark were having dinner in the Hotel with Pastor Sally and her husband Chris the weekend before Christmas and spotted Clayton and Valerie carrying beautiful, heavy-looking leather bags into the Hotel lobby and heading for the elevators without looking around. "They must have done a lot of shopping!"

CHAPTER FIFTEEN

Pieces of Silver

A surprise donation to the Historical Society just before Christmas had Mitzi feeling like a young child receiving that special gift from Santa. She received funding to acquire several pieces of silver that had been made in Bethlehem by a Moravian silversmith in the mid-1700's. The silver would be going up for auction right after the holidays.

Years ago, Vaughn's parents had taken Mitzi and Vaughn to their favorite antique shop in Connecticut. The shop owner and very reputable antiques dealer, Michael Brown, had struck up a friendship with Mitzi from their first meeting. They loved discussing historic houses and their contents. He would always call or email to keep Mitzi up to date on the latest news in the antiques world. Mitzi called to ask him to look at the silver pieces that were coming up for auction and verify their authenticity. She was very conservative with the Society's finances and always wanted an independent opinion before purchasing artifacts for the collection.

Michael casually mentioned that all the major dealers in the northeast received a very unusual message from the FBI to be on the lookout for any one showing an unusual amount of interest in heirloom jewelry. "Mitzi, I don't think you have much in your collection."

"Michael, you are correct. We have very few pieces of jewelry in our collection since most of our families pass those family treasures along to the next generation. The jewelry we have does not have any great value."

"Well, just be on the look out for any international jewel thieves," he said jokingly.

"What do they look like? How are you supposed to know what to look for?"

"No one really knows."

"I wonder what they are looking for exactly?"

"Possibly rare diamonds."

"This is definitely making your Christmas more exciting with all the beautiful antique jewelry you have in your shop."

"Maybe they are headed your way, not to Connecticut!"

"What would they want here? We don't have anything like that in our museum or historic sites. People have donated many fabulous things, but not rare jewels! You are just being silly trying to get me upset."

"No, I am really serious. Be careful. I know that you and your friend Adele like to play amateur detective all the time!"

"Oh my goodness, I wonder if they are actually here in Bethlehem. There is a drop dead gorgeous couple that has been staying in the hotel here off and on during the past several weeks. Adele thought she saw a glint of a gun when we were on the bus and maybe we were right to be suspicious. I will notify our local FBI office. But I still don't know what they would want here..."

"Remember, your mystery couple may simply be tourists enjoying Christmas in Bethlehem. Be careful Mitzi, you don't want a lawsuit on your hands."

After hanging up the phone, Mitzi stared out the window of her office. Could Clayton and Valerie really be international jewel thieves? Here in Bethlehem? It was just too fantastic!

CHAPTER SIXTEEN

The Christmas Pageant

EACH year on the Saturday morning before Christmas, the town celebrated with a Live Christmas Pageant on Sand Island. There were real camels, sheep, cows, and townspeople dressed as shepherds, Mary, Joseph, and the baby, angels and Wise Men.

It was such a wonderful expression of the season. Thousands of people congregated on Sand Island to participate. Most of the tourists had gone home and it was now time for the community to come together to celebrate the season.

Adele and Zeke, Mitzi and Vaughn, Beth and Mark, Rodrigo and Fred and their families were all joining in on the experience.

As the pageant was about to begin, Mitzi whispered to Adele that Roger had told her that his girlfriend saw Clayton and Valerie back in town. Beth turned to say quietly that she and Mark had also seen them the night before, while having dinner at the Hotel.

Just then Mark spotted Clayton and Valerie and waved to them across the crowd, but they did not seem friendly and really avoided looking at him during the pageant. Mark whispered to Beth "What's up with them, after we bumped into them at that new restaurant and had such a nice time at dinner? They have always been so friendly with us." "Shhhh," came from the elderly lady behind them.

Beth noticed that they were carrying Historical Society shopping bags. I wonder what happened to their leather bags she thought.

As the crowd was dispersing after the pageant, Mark and Beth decided to try to follow Clayton and Valerie, but all of a sudden they seemed to disappear into thin air.

"They are not ghosts." Where did they go?

Eventually, Beth and Mark stopped looking. Obviously, their new-found "friends" were avoiding them.

As Mitzi, Vaughn, Adele, and Zeke started walking back to Church Street, Adele got a frantic call from CJ, the Church Sexton, "Someone broke into the CE Building! The whole putz is destroyed!"

"The entire putz destroyed? Call the police. I'll be right there. This is a disaster. The putz always reopens right after the pageant. It's a family tradition to go putzing together."

Hearing what happened, Mitzi said to Adele, "We'll open the museums' putzes and direct people there instead. I'll call my staff to organize it."

When they walked into the CE Building, they were in disbelief at what they encountered. The rocks and moss were on the floor, the logs and drift wood broken into many pieces, and the figures were strewn all over the room. A complete disaster!

Zeke said, "Obviously, the pageant proved to be a diversion. When everyone was down there, no one was here. But the CE Building was locked and alarmed wasn't it?"

"Yes, absolutely, of course!" retorted Adele, somewhat defensively.

"How could someone get in?" asked Vaughn, trying to diffuse the situation.

Just then the police arrived and started to take statements from Adele and CJ.

"No one is allowed to touch anything until we check for any finger prints," instructed the same young officer who recognized Mitzi from the late-night false alarm ride to the Moravian Museum across the Church Green. "We will need you to identify anything missing."

Unaware of the excitement going on at the CE Building, Mark and Beth walked to their home a few blocks from Sand Island. The door bell rang just after they got back from the Live Pageant. Beth called from the kitchen, "Mark, will you get the door?" As Mark opened the door, he was surprised to see Clayton and Valerie on their doorstep with packages.

"Hope we are not interrupting, but we wanted to drop off a few gifts for your new house that we brought back from New York. We tried to avoid you and Beth at the pageant, because we had the gifts with us and didn't want to ruin the surprise."

"Beth, guess who's here? It's Clayton and Valerie bearing gifts!"

"Please have them come in," Beth said as she was drying her hands on her apron. "I was just starting to make some Christmas cookies. Sorry for the mess."

As the two young couples sat in the living room enjoying each other's company, the conversation turned to Christmas Day.

"Will you be going back to New York for Christmas?"

"No, we just fell in love with Bethlehem at Christmastime; it seems to be like a Norman Rockwell painting. We can't get enough of the charm. We have been spending as much of our vacation this past month here as we could," said Valerie.

"That's certainly true!" added Clayton. "She has had us visiting every putz in town, several times over!"

"You see, when I was a little girl," Valerie began to explain, "my grandmother was from the Czech Republic and came to this country. At Christmas, the entire family, my aunts and uncles and cousins, all of the family went to her house on Christmas Eve. And I remember clearly that we grandchildren were allowed to go into this one room, and we had to be very quiet in that room. And there was this wonderful display, a Nativity scene, no, the whole Christmas story was set out for us to see. It was amazing. As little children we were all wide-eyed and spellbound. And I remember that my aunt had to hold up my littlest cousin so that she could see everything. And of course, we were not allowed to touch anything! You can imagine for us little ones, what a temptation!" Everyone laughed as Valerie continued.

"I didn't know until I was older that what my grandmother set up every Christmas was called a 'putz' and that here in Bethlehem every Christmas you all do the same."

"We Moravians have been doing the 'putz thing' for a long time!" injected Beth. "A very long time!"

"So when I saw that they were here to see in Bethlehem, I had to keep going back to see them again and again. I guess I was trying to relive my childhood at my grandmother's house. Is that silly?"

"Oh no," exclaimed Beth. "I think it is a wonderful story. A wonderful Christmas story. So where will you be spending Christmas?"

"We are staying at Hotel Bethlehem, so we will be having Christmas dinner there."

"Oh, heavens, you need to be with family and friends for the holiday," exclaimed Beth, "not having dinner alone in the Hotel."

"Both of our families are out on the West Coast and we need to be back in New York to prepare for a New Year's Eve fashion shoot the day after the holiday since we've taken the last month off for vacation."

In the Christmas spirit, Beth, almost instinctively said, "You must have Christmas dinner with us. I insist!"

Mark added, "Beth's mother Elaine and her new husband Merrill will be here and I'm sure you'll enjoy hearing their stories of old Bethlehem."

CHAPTER SEVENTEEN

A New Day

THE next day when the crime scene was released, Adele enlisted the Putz Committee and Mitzi got Fred and Rodrigo to help clean up and investigate to see if any pieces were missing. After hours of work, sorting through the broken drift wood and ruined moss, the volunteers were able to make sense of the mess. Even with a number of broken figures, they were able to recreate each scene of the putz. Amazingly, there were only six pieces actually missing - three Wise Men and three camels.

Mitzi exclaimed "Adele, aren't those the new pieces you told me about? The ones from Germany? The ones in the package that Baxter brought to the Church office? Did you ever find out who sent them?"

"No, no one ever contacted us about that package. This is unbelievable. This is just unbelievable. I have to call the police right now."

"While you handle that with the police, I will help here wherever I can."

News of the incident spread quickly throughout the area. Almost before the committee could clean up the CE Building, concerned citizens, Moravians and non-Moravians alike, were bringing fresh moss from the Poconos, driftwood from their own families' trips to the beach last summer and putz figures from other churches. The community was coming together in the spirit of the season. The putz would be ready once again for the annual visit of children on Christmas Eve.

Meanwhile, Mitzi's docents in costume walked around the Church Green directing visitors to the putzes in the Moravian Museum and the Single Sisters' House and handed out directions to the other Moravian Church putzes in Bethlehem.

CHAPTER EIGHTEEN

The Police Report

THE Church office received a most unusual phone call. "Adele, the police are on the phone," said a nervous Margaret.

As Adele hung up the phone, she grabbed her coat and walked the two blocks to City Hall. All the way, she wondered how this could be happening two days before Christmas.

"From the evidence, we believe that someone must have been hiding in the CE building when it was closed and alarmed for the night. There was no sign of a break-in. The next morning when everyone was at the pageant, the robbery took place. The robber used the pageant as a diversion."

Oh my goodness, Zeke was right, thought Adele.

During the interview, the police asked Adele how someone would be able to get into the building if the alarm was on. She could only think of one thing - the old tunnels.

Apparently, the robber or robbers must have found the old tunnel dating from the early days of the community. There was always talk by the guys on the Putz Committee, who kidded about the old tunnels that were thought to be used for safety from attack during the French and Indian War. One of the tunnels ran from the Single Sisters' House to what would become the CE Building. It was converted into use by the utility company when the building was constructed about one hundred years ago.

The police continued to explain that finger prints led them to a Jack Clark whose prints were on file. He was an international antiques dealer out of New York. There was some connection to a Bethlehem widow, Catherine Mary Churok who lived at 61 East Church Street. The police believed that she was his sister-in-law.

Adele was shocked. "That's Stevie's mother!" She went on to explain the boy's involvement with the missing camels from other putzes. The person who got Stevie Churok to steal the camels was, after all, his very own uncle.

The police continued, "From what we can tell and from what you told us about that package, this Jack Clark must have arranged to have it mailed to Catherine, but it got delivered to the Widows' House at 61 West Church Street by mistake. We interviewed her and she told us he was on his way back to New York. He was picked up somewhere in New Jersey on the interstate and the officers found a treasure of uncut diamonds in the hollowed out heavy putz figures. His finger prints on the Wise Men and camels matched what we found in your CE Building."

Later that day when Adele told Mitzi the whole story, Mitzi thought, "Oh my goodness. Michael Brown was right. An international jewel thief right here in Bethlehem!"

When Mitzi called Michael to tell him about the putz caper, she invited him, and his partner Pat to spend Christmas with her and Vaughn in Bethlehem.

CHAPTER NINETEEN

A Very Merry Christmas

The second Christmas in their new house was a memorable one for Mark and Beth. Not only was the house in better shape this year, but their Christmas dinner with Beth's mother and new step-father Merrill had an added element with the attendance of their new friends, Clayton and Valerie. They shared a traditional family dinner together.

With the excitement of the putz caper finally over, Mitzi and Vaughn had a wonderful Christmas dinner with their company from Connecticut, Michael and Pat and Vaughn's parents, Brett and Cecilia. All the museums were closed, the Visitor Center shut down for the day, and there were no tours. Mitzi could relax - at least she hoped that there would be no false alarms.

On the other side of town, Adele and Zeke were sharing dinner with their children and grandchildren after a wild morning of gift exchange and playing with new toys left by Santa. The busy Christmas Eve Vigil services attended by thousands of members, friends, and visitors were finally over, and now just a warm memory. A guest preacher took part in the Christmas Day service that morning so that Adele could have a break from preparing a message.

As a gentle snow began to fall on the little town of Bethlehem, a tall, slender docent wearing a woolen cape, her haube peeking out from under the hood and white ribbons barely showing, closed the cape around her from the evening chill. She walked quietly along Church Street alone, past the Moravian Museum with its single candle reflecting in every window and turned the corner in front of Central Moravian Church with its Advent Star shining brightly from the belfry in the darkness of this Christmas night.

Choir system - A form of communal living in early Bethlehem in which members of a particular group resided, worked and worshipped together. Single Sisters, for example, lived in the Single Sisters' House, independent of their families.

Christmas Putz - From the German word, *putzen*, meaning to clean or to decorate, a putz depicts the story of the birth of Jesus through miniature putz figures arranged in various biblical scenes.

Docent - A tour guide; a woman or man who interprets history for visitors.

Haube - A traditional form-fitting white head covering worn by Moravian women in the 1700's to the mid 1800's. Also called a Schneppelhaube, (Schneppel meaning 'beak,') it featured a beak-like point at the forehead.

Moravian Star - A multi-pointed star first made in Niesky, Germany in 1820/21 by Christian Madsen of Herrnhut, Germany. The stars were produced commercially in 1897 in Herrnhut, where they are still made and sold today. Moravian Stars are hung on the first Sunday in Advent. In America the traditional color is white, but the star is also made in various colors such as blue, yellow, red and orange.

"Morning Star, O Cheering Sight" - A beloved antiphonal hymn written in 1836 by Francis F. Hagen, sung by the congregation and child soloist on Christmas Eve.

Nativity - Referring to the Gospel stories about the birth of Jesus.

Historic Bethlehem Museums & Sites

HISTORIC Bethlehem Museums & Sites (HBMS) is a 501(c)(3) nonprofit organization that formed in 1993 to consolidate the operations of several local museums and historic sites. Historic Bethlehem Museums & Sites interprets three centuries of the history and culture of Bethlehem from its founding as a Moravian community in 1741 to the 21st century through tours, exhibits and programs.

Historic Bethlehem Museums & Sites maintains 20 historic buildings and sites in Bethlehem.

The Moravian Museum of Bethlehem includes the 1741 Gemeinhaus, the 1752 Apothecary and herb garden, the 1744/1752 Single Sisters' House, and the 1758/1765 Nain-Schober House.

The Colonial Industrial Quarter, America's earliest industrial park situated on a 10 acre site, includes the 1762 Waterworks, the 1761 Tannery, 1750 Smithy (reconstructed), 1780/1830 Miller's House, 1869 Luckenbach Mill, 1750s Springhouse (reconstructed), and the archeological remains of the 1740s Pottery, 1770s Dye House, 1750s Butchery, and 1700s Oil Mill.

The 1810 Goundie House and Visitor Center is housed in the 1830s Schropp Shop on Main Street.

The 1748/1848 Burnside Plantation, a 6.5 acre farm in the city, includes the 1748/1818 farmhouse, 1820s summer kitchen and corncrib, 1840s wagon shed and two 1840s bank barns, one with the only operating high horse-powered wheel in the U.S., a kitchen garden, an apple orchard, and two meadows.

The Kemerer Museum of Decorative Arts, housed in three interconnected mid-1800s homes, features changing exhibits, period rooms, and galleries with furniture, paintings, china, clothing, silver and doll house collection highlighting over three centuries of decorative arts. This museum speaks to the changes in style and design over the years.

HBMS has over 60,000 artifacts in its combined collections. In addition, the HBMS Library and Archives has 10,000 photographs, thousands of documents, letters, maps related to the history of Bethlehem, and a 2,000 volume library.

In 2003, Historic Bethlehem Museums & Sites became a founding member of the International Moravian Heritage Network, one of six key 18th century historic Moravian communities worldwide.

In 2004, HBMS was named an affiliate of the Smithsonian Institution, one of only 180 museums in the United States to receive this honor.

Website: www.historicbethlehem.org

Historic Moravian Bethlehem

IN 2012, Historic Moravian Bethlehem was designated a National Historic Landmark District by the U.S. Secretary of the Interior. It encompasses just over 14 acres in the heart of the City of Bethlehem within the Central Bethlehem National Register Historic District.

It was here in 1741 at the confluence of the Monocacy Creek and the Lehigh River that the first Moravians felled white oak trees and began building their community on a 500 acre tract purchased in the spring. They located their crafts, trades, and industries along the waterways and their institutional dwellings on the limestone bluff above.

The earliest structures were built of hewn logs. The first house is no longer extant; however, the second structure known as the 1741 Gemeinhaus (National Historic Landmark) is still standing and houses the Moravian Museum of Bethlehem. A majority of the 18th century German Colonial style stone structures remain including the 1744-1772 Bell House/Sisters' House Complex, 1748 Single Brethren's House, 1751 Old Chapel, 1761 Tannery, 1762 Waterworks (National Historic Landmark), 1768 Widows' House, 1782-1834 Miller's House, and the archeological remains of the butchery, dye house, pottery, and oil mill. In the center of the District is the 1803-1806 Central Moravian Church built in the Federal style. A contributing property to the District is the 1810 Goundie House, one of the earliest brick homes in the Federal architectural style.

The Moravians in Bethlehem lived in a communal society organized into groups, called choirs, segregated by age, gender, and marital status. The society also operated under a General Economy where everyone worked for the good of the community and received care from cradle to grave. Based on their societal organization, the community developed large institutional choir houses, superb examples of German Colonial style architecture in America.

Historic Moravian Bethlehem encompasses excellent examples of the architecture and town planning of the 18th century community. Today, a Moravian from the mid-1700s would recognize their community and feel at home walking the streets of this part of the City of Bethlehem. Many of these buildings have been in continuous use since they were constructed and some for their original purpose.

Central Moravian Church

BETHLEHEM was founded by members of the Moravian Church and named on December 24, 1741, by their leader Count Nicholas Ludwig von Zinzendorf. As the early community outgrew its worship spaces, the 1741 Gemeinhaus Saal, as well as the 1751 Old Chapel, a third place of worship was needed. Central Moravian Church was built between 1803 and 1806 to accommodate 1,500 people at a time when the total population of Bethlehem was only 580. Today, the seating capacity is 1,100.

Without interior pillars, the heavy roof and belfry are supported by 68-foot-long white oak timbers whose ends rest on the side walls rising from massive foundations. From the iconic belfry, the Bethlehem Area Moravians' Trombone Choir, the oldest brass choir in continuous existence in the United States, announces the deaths of members of the congregation, as well as festivals of the church and community. The belfry houses the oldest working American-made tower clock, built in Bethlehem in 1747. The current bell was hung in 1868.

The Moravians brought an outstanding musical culture with them to America, and Central Moravian Church became known as one of the most prestigious places for music. Haydn's oratorio, *The Creation*, was performed for the first time in America in Central Moravian Church in 1811. The first American performance of Bach's complete *Mass in B Minor* was also held in Central Moravian Church in 1900. The latter earned the church status as a National Landmark of Music. USA Today, December 18, 1998, named Central Moravian Church one of the nation's "Ten Great Places to Reflect on Christmas Eve."

Through the years, Central Moravian Church has been the spiritual home of noteworthy musicians, scientists, craftspeople, writers, poets, artists, physicians, educators, and civic leaders. Today, worship services are held on Sundays at 9 a.m. in the Old Chapel and at 11 a.m. in the Sanctuary. Summer worship (June-August) is at 10 a.m.

Website: www.centralmoravianchurch.org

Moravian Denomination

THE Moravian Church had its origin in the pre-Reformation awakening under Jan Hus. The Church was organized formally as the *Unitas Fratrum*, the Unity of the Brethren, in 1457. Because much of its early history centered in Moravia, now part of the Czech Republic, the Unity became known as the Moravian Church. The Moravian Church was renewed in Herrnhut, Germany, in 1727, and is recognized as one of the oldest organized Protestant denominations in the world.

The Old Moravian Chapel

THE Old Moravian Chapel was constructed in 1751 as the second place of worship for the Moravian Congregation of Bethlehem. Originally, the Chapel could be entered only from the Gemeinhaus and Bell House, with the men and women entering through separate doors. The Communion Table (pulpit area) was on the west wall instead of the south wall as it is today. In 1865, the Chapel was altered and an entrance was added on the north wall.

Many notable people worshiped in the Chapel during the Revolutionary War period, including Benjamin Franklin, Martha Washington, George Washington; also John Adams, Samuel Adams, Marquis de Lafayette, John Hancock, Ethan Allen, Count Casimir Pulaski, General Horatio Gates and John Paul Jones.

On March 10, 1792, fifty one chiefs and representatives of the Six-Nations (Iroquois Confederacy) came to Bethlehem on their way to Philadelphia to meet with George Washington. Among them were the great chiefs Red Jacket, Corn Planter and Big Tree. They gathered in the Chapel, the Indians in ceremonial feathers and leggings and the brethren and sisters in their plain garb.

The Old Chapel is used for early worship on Sunday, weddings, funerals and special musical programs during Advent and Lent. Moravian Academy uses the Chapel for weekly services and other special events.

The Moravian Archives

THE Moravian Archives is the official repository for the records of the Moravian Church in America - Northern Province. The Northern Province covers the Moravian churches in the United States (except for North Carolina, Florida, Georgia and Virginia) and Canada. Records from the Moravian Church in Alaska, Labrador, Nicaragua and the Eastern West-Indies can also be found in the Archives.

Located in a modern 9,200 square foot building with two climate-controlled vaults, the Moravian Archives contains approximately 8,000 linear feet of material.

Documents stored in the Archives provide the history of the province beginning in 1740 and include records of many congregations. There are over 1,000,000 pages written in 18th-century German script, large numbers of English-language documents, over 20,000 printed volumes and thousands of pamphlets, paintings, prints, maps, and photographs as well as selected personal papers.

The Archives is open Monday through Friday, 8 a.m. to 4:30 p.m.
Website: www.moravianchurcharchives.org

Bethlehem Area Moravians, Inc.

BETHLEHEM Area Moravians, Inc., had its beginnings in the old Moravian Congregation of Bethlehem. The original Congregation was comprised of three local churches: Central, College Hill and West Side Moravian Churches. At one point, Edgeboro Moravian Church was also a part of the Congregation.

Together, members of the Congregation gathered to celebrate Christmas Eve, Children's Lovefeast in September, Easter Dawn and the Anniversary of the founding of the Congregation on June 25, 1742. The organization was governed by a General Board of Elders and a General Board of Trustees, whose responsibilities paralleled that of individual church boards.

During the 250th anniversary year of 1992, Bethlehem Area Moravians, Inc. was formed and now includes Central, College Hill, West Side, Edgeboro, East Hills and Advent Moravian Churches. "BAM" serves and ministers to people in the Bethlehem community, especially through housing. A number of Moravian Houses have been developed for those who qualify because of particular needs.

Moravian Village, a continuing care retirement community sponsored by BAM, provides comfortable and secure living for older adults.

Moravian College Housing, also known as the HILL, is a living and learning residence for 231 Moravian College students. This facility is sponsored by BAM and provides a comfortable, safe and superior learning environment.

For Further Reading

Caldwell, Douglas W. and Reifinger, Carol A. *Let Us Go Over to Bethlehem: A Guide to the Moravian Community.* Bethlehem, PA: Central Moravian Church, 2007.

Hamilton, Kenneth G. *Church Street in Old Bethlehem.* Bethlehem, PA: Moravian Congregation of Bethlehem, 1988.

Howland, Garth A. *An Architectural History of the Moravian Church.* Bethlehem, PA: Times Publishing Co., 1947.

Huetter, Karen Zerbe. *The Bethlehem Waterworks.* Bethlehem, PA: Historic Bethlehem, Inc., 1976.

LeCount, Charles A. *The Blacksmiths of Early Bethlehem.* Bethlehem, PA: 1992.

Levering, Joseph Mortimer. *A History of Bethlehem, Pennsylvania 1741-1892.* Bethlehem, PA: Times Publishing Company, 1903.

Mowers, Charlene Donchez and Carol A. Reifinger. *The Body in the Vat: Tales from the Tannery.* Bethlehem, PA: Christmas City Printing, 2014.

Nelson, Vernon H. *The Bethlehem Gemeinhaus.* Bethlehem, PA: Moravian Congregation of Bethlehem, 1990.

Schwarz, Ralph Grayson. *Bethlehem on the Lehigh.* Bethlehem, PA: Bethlehem Area Foundation, 1991.

Sweitzer, Vangie Roby. *Christmas In Bethlehem: A Moravian Heritage.* Bethlehem, PA: Central Moravian Church, 2000.

—. *The Moravian Christmas Putz.* Bethlehem, PA: Central Moravian Church, 2013.

__. *Tuned for Praise: The Bethlehem Area Moravian Trombone Choir, 1754-2004.* Bethlehem, PA: Central Moravian Church, 2004.

Visit, Explore, Experience Historic Moravian Bethlehem, Pennsylvania. Bethlehem, PA: Historic Bethlehem Museums & Sites, 2014.

About the Authors

CHARLENE DONCHEZ MOWERS is President of Historic Bethlehem Museums & Sites. A native of Bethlehem, she has been involved in preserving and interpreting the history of this community for over 20 years.

She serves on the Discover Lehigh Valley Board of Directors and the Bethlehem Council of the Greater Lehigh Valley Chamber of Commerce. She served as co-chair of the Lehigh Valley Industrial Heritage Coalition and is a representative to the International Moravian Heritage Network. She chairs the Archives Committee of Moravian Academy. She has been a guest speaker at preservation and museum-related conferences, including the Pennsylvania Federation of Museums and Historical Organizations, Preservation Pennsylvania, Smithsonian Institution, and the international Moravian Heritage Network Conferences.

Previously, she chaired the Bethlehem Tourism Authority Board, served on the Christkindlmarkt Council and the Board of Trustees of Moravian Academy, and was a library volunteer at the Allentown Art Museum.

She has a B.A. from Arcadia University and an M.A. from Temple University. She is a Distinguished Alumna of Moravian Academy. She and her husband reside in Bethlehem.

Along with co-author Carol A. Reifinger, she wrote *The Body in the Vat: Tales from the Tannery.*

CAROL A. REIFINGER retired as Senior Pastor of Central Moravian Church after twenty-eight years in ministry. She received her Master of Divinity Degree from Moravian Theological Seminary in 1984.

As a Pastor of Central Moravian Church, she served Bethlehem Area Moravians, Inc., from its inception, as an Executive Board member, as Vice President, and as Ministries Committee Chair. Part of her work with the Board was to develop the Moravian Village Continuing Care Retirement Community, which was sponsored by Bethlehem Area Moravians, Inc.

She co-authored the book, *Let Us Go Over to Bethlehem, A Guide to the Moravian Community*, with her former colleague, the late Rev. Dr. Douglas W. Caldwell. Along with Charlene Donchez Mowers, she wrote *The Body in the Vat: Tales from the Tannery.*

She is enjoying a busy retirement as a volunteer at the Moravian Archives and Central Church's Star and Candle Shoppe. She lives in Bethlehem with her husband, Jim.

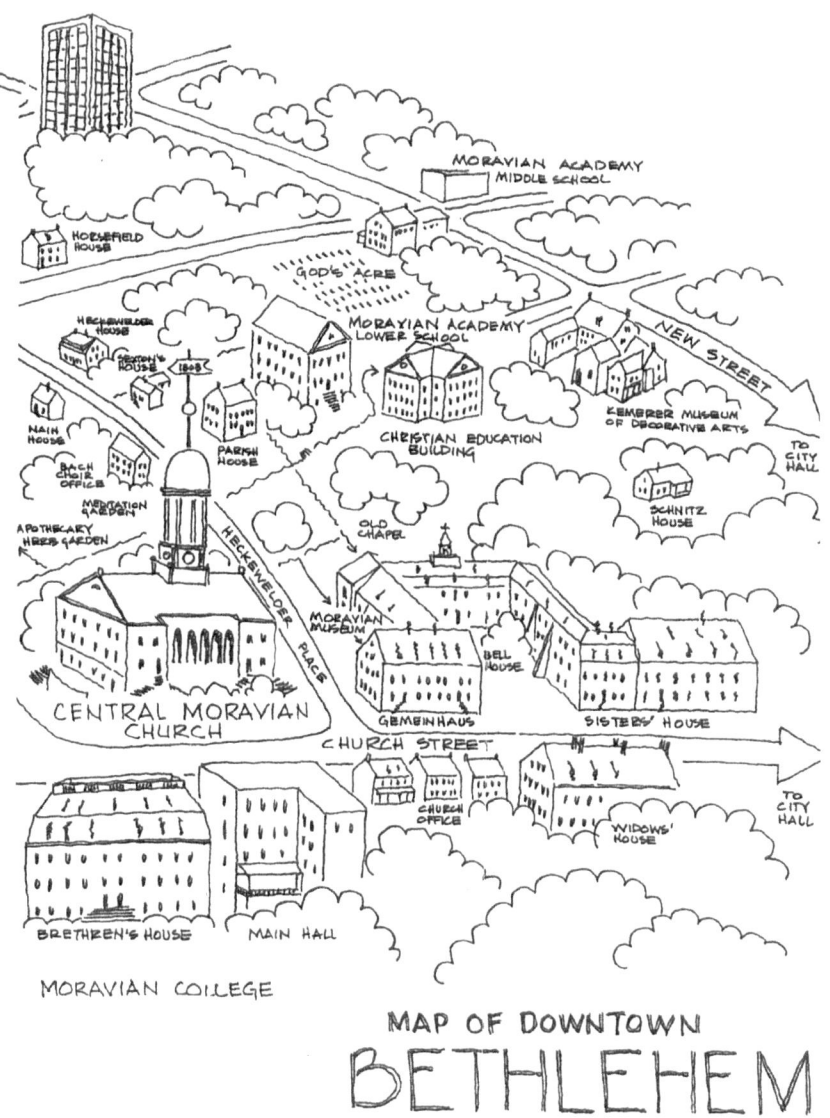

MAP OF DOWNTOWN
BETHLEHEM